THE

LAST

STRIPTEASE

THE

LAST

STRIPTEASE

MICHAEL

WILEY

THOMAS DUNNE BOOKS/ST. MARTIN'S MINOTAUR ≋ NEW YORK

This is a work of fiction. All of the characters, organizations, and events portrayed in this novel are either products of the author's imagination or are used fictitiously.

THOMAS DUNNE BOOKS.
An imprint of St. Martin's Press.

www.thomasdunnebooks.com
www.minotaurbooks.com

Design by Dylan Rosal Greif

Library of Congress Cataloging-in-Publication Data

Wiley, Michael, 1961–
　　The last striptease / Michael Wiley. — 1st ed.
　　　　p.　cm.
　　ISBN-13: 978-0-312-37250-7
　　ISBN-10: 0-312-37250-7
　　1. Private investigators—Illinois—Chicago—Fiction.
2. Judges—Crimes against—Fiction.　I. Title.
　　PS3623.I5433L37　2007
　　813'.6—dc22

2007021541

First Edition: October 2007

10　9　8　7　6　5　4　3　2　1

To Julie, Isaac, Maya, and Elias,
who keep me laughing

ACKNOWLEDGMENTS

Julia Burns, David Knowles, Sam Kimball, and Peter Wiley have listened to my stories (repeatedly) and have told me unerringly when to stop and when to go. SJ Rozan has read my work the way I hope all will read it and has shown me great kindness and generosity of spirit. Bob Randisi and the PWA have welcomed me in and given me dinner; there's no better table than theirs. At St. Martin's Press, Ruth Cavin has offered me the invaluable gift of her good words and sharp editorial eye, and Toni Plummer has guided me confidently down many new trails. I would be lost without all of you.

ONE

NORTH DEARBORN, A COUPLE blocks off the Gold Coast high-rises, is a high-priced neighborhood, full of forty-year-old guys fresh out of divorces from suburban wives. Guys with good money from good jobs or okay money from okay jobs and dreams of an easy life interrupted only by vigorous sex after years of cutting the backyard grass every summer weekend. If they've got money, they buy a Jaguar or a Mercedes convertible, which they keep in a garage. If they don't, a scooter or a moped, which they keep in the front vestibule of their apartment building. But after a couple months, their sports cars stay parked in the garage, and their scooters and mopeds collect dust in the vestibules, and most of the year is winter in Chicago anyway, so the guys work their good jobs or their okay jobs, then go home and climb upstairs to their apartments and cook a microwave dinner. Afterward, they go to bed early or they walk out to the bars on Rush Street and get drunk with other guys like themselves.

I know because I looked at apartments in the neighborhood after Corrine and I split up. I didn't rent because I didn't like what the neighborhood told me about myself. Sometimes denial is good. For me, it's dessert every night after a microwave dinner.

I try to avoid the area, but on a warm Monday night in September, I sat in my car across the street from a store called Stoyz. Lots of neon, about a third of it dead, and a front window covered with a chrome finish, so you could see your reflection from outside. The kind of place you would think would get run out of a high-priced neighborhood, except it served a need.

A man named Ahmed Hassan ran the store. Mr. Hassan had stopped paying child support, and my lawyer, Larry Weiss, who also represented Hassan's ex-wife, asked me to track him down and deliver a court summons. Sometimes when business is slow, I do favors for Larry. Sometimes when business gets too fast and lands me in jail, he does favors for me. No money exchanged. Business was slow, so the court summons and a photograph of Hassan sat on the passenger seat. It was chiseler work. Not what I do. But here I was, and I'd been to plenty of places like this before.

I watched the storefront. A glowing red sign advertising Stoyz jutted out from the brick wall above the door. A smaller purple one advertised cigarettes, videos, magazines, and accessories. More red said the store was open. The chrome window faced the street like a stone drunk who wouldn't tell you what was inside his head no matter how many times you slapped him. But I figured Hassan was in there behind the counter.

A white van was parked in the dark outside the store, and a deliveryman in a brown jumpsuit, work gloves, and a yellow baseball cap was unloading boxes from the back. I would wait until the guy finished the delivery and left; then I would present the summons to Hassan. No reason to rile Hassan by making it public.

The deliveryman stacked three boxes on a dolly, balanced a fourth on his shoulder, and backed the load into the store through the door. On the neon sign, the purple z in the word *magazines* flickered; soon it would burn out. Then the other letters would burn out, one by one, until the store sat in total darkness. And then, if we were lucky, the store itself would disappear, taking Hassan with it. The world wouldn't be any worse off.

A sheet of newspaper blew across the street, tumbling like the ghost of an animal that hadn't lived in this city for 150 years. Or like a tumbleweed. And I was John Wayne or Gary Cooper or whoever. But I heard no twanging Western music.

I heard a gunshot. It exploded dully inside the store.

The newspaper came to a rest in the gutter.

Two more gunshots exploded.

The deliveryman ran out. No boxes, no dolly. He ran scared. His muscles didn't move him as fast as he wanted to go. He scrambled into the white van, and it skidded from the curb. The van clipped the bumper of the car parked in front of it and disappeared down the street.

I grabbed my cell phone and punched 911. Before the

dispatcher answered, I had my Glock out of the glove compartment and I'd checked the clip.

"Gunshots," I shouted, and I gave the dispatcher the address of Stoyz.

"Who is shooting?" she asked. Calm, like I was reporting a lost cat.

Halfway out the car door, I didn't bother to answer.

"Please stay on the line," she said.

I threw the phone on the passenger seat and ran across to the store.

Only one person was inside. A tall man, fat as a potato. He groped along a display case, head down, smearing the glass with blood. He passed a closed cash register. He passed a door, open to a supply room. He had on white khakis and sleek black Italian loafers. His shirt was sky blue silk, stained with sweat and blood. His head was round and heavy and shaved bald. Even with his face against the glass, I recognized him as Ahmed Hassan.

He stopped moving, and his muscles tensed, his fingers digging at the display glass like the hookahs inside could save his life. A spasm shot through his body and the glass shattered. The wooden legs gave way, and the case collapsed to the floor under him. He fell, soft as a bag of potatoes.

He needed help quick, but I didn't like the door open to the supply room behind him and the chance that the shooter was in there.

I ducked behind the display counter, waited, listened to silence, moved to the supply room door. A bullet had splintered the door frame. I swung my Glock into the room and followed it. Except for some metal shelves holding cleaning supplies and electronic equipment, the room was empty. A steel door stood open to an alley behind the store. I closed and bolted it.

Hassan was moaning. I went to him and turned him onto his back. He had two neat puncture wounds where he'd taken bullets: one in his neck, one in his chest. The wound in his neck pulsed blood like a fountain. Broken glass jutted out of cuts on his face. Blood pooled in his eyes. He didn't blink. He was already beyond seeing.

"Mr. Hassan," I said.

He didn't answer. He was beyond hearing, too.

"Who shot you?"

He moaned.

I tried again. "Who—"

He grabbed upward blindly and got my arm, didn't let go.

I would stay with him, letting him clutch my arm, until the cops or an ambulance arrived. If he died before they came, I would let him die holding on to someone. A stranger was better than no one.

"Patti?" he mumbled.

Patti, his ex-wife, was suing him for child support. Did she shoot him? Or was he already half out of this world and regretting what he'd left unloved and uncared for? Maybe if he survived, he would start paying child support without a judge telling him to. I tried again. "Who shot you?"

He didn't answer.

His grip on my arm weakened. His hand fell to the floor like it had to, like everything has to, and he didn't lift it again. He lay there, breathing hard. Another spasm passed through his body. The blood pulsed slowly from his neck. Nothing I could do unless I put a tourniquet around his throat.

And then he was quiet. I listened anyway. Sirens howled in the distance.

TWO

WHEN TWO UNIFORMED COPS came into the store, I was sitting on the carpet, sorting through a box the deliveryman had dropped. It was the only box in the place. The other three that the deliveryman had been carrying were missing. So was his dolly. And the deliveryman had left empty-handed. The cops were clean-cut rookies, a short, skinny boy and a tall, beefy girl, wide-eyed and so scared that you could blow at them and they would either dive to the ground or shoot you dead, equal chance either way, so I sat still and didn't breathe. They swung their guns left and right like flashlights with beams that would light up a murky darkness, though the overhead fluorescent was plenty bright. When the boy cop saw Ahmed Hassan's body lying in the broken glass, he swung his gun at him so fast, I thought he was going to shoot another hole in him.

"He's dead," I said.

The partner leveled her gun at me, slower, but with a finger on the trigger.

"And I'm the one who called nine one one."

That didn't impress them.

"Lie facedown on the floor," she said.

I raised my hands and gave her a friendly smile. "I'm a private detective, and I called you. I don't know what's living on this floor, but I don't want my face in it."

The boy cop swung his gun on me and shouted, "Put your fucking face on the floor!"

"You know that you spit when you yell?" I said, but I did as I was told.

He held his gun on me while his partner made sure no one was hiding in the rest of the store. When she came back, I told her, "My detective's license is in my wallet, front left pocket. And I'm carrying a gun, also left side, inside the jacket."

News of the gun made the boy step back, but the girl cop cuffed my hands, took my Glock, patted me down for other weapons, and took my wallet. She had big shoulders and big hips and was big in between. Her name tag said she was Elle Samuelson, but aside from the name and a little blond ponytail, she didn't look anything like a supermodel. I smiled, friendly, but she glanced at me as if I were a bug on the floor, then rifled through my wallet. When she saw my detective's license, she shot a look at her partner. "His name's Joseph Kozmarski. He's a PI."

The partner kept his weapon pointed at my head and

shrugged. "We've got a victim with gunshot wounds and a man with a gun." He looked smug like he'd done some hard math.

Car doors slammed outside and a megaphone crackled. The boy cop grinned when four more uniformed cops came in through the front door, followed by a fat, balding detective in civvies. The boy probably saw a promotion in me lying on the floor in handcuffs.

The detective stepped around the uniformed cops and looked the place over. He shook his head at Hassan's body, sighed deep and sad. Then he glanced at me. He tilted his head and looked confused. He walked over slowly, the way you approach a dog that sometimes bites. He wedged a brown shoe under my shoulder and lifted his foot. I rolled with it and landed on my back.

The detective cocked his head again and gave a big toothy grin.

I cocked my head and grinned, too.

"Hey, Joe," he said.

"Hey, Bill."

"How's stuff?"

"You know, a little slow. You?"

"Busy. Don't get home enough. How's your mom?"

I shrugged. "She'll never change."

"Change is overrated."

"How's Eileen?"

"She's doing good," he said. "She wants me to ask you for dinner."

"Anytime."

"Friday?"

"Friday's good."

He nodded. "Great to see you, Joe."

"You too, Bill."

He let his grin fade. "Didn't you show them your license?"

I nodded at the girl cop. "She's got it."

"Then why have they got you like this?"

I shrugged.

He turned to the boy cop and whispered, "Get this man out of these cuffs." The look on the cop's face said he'd stopped hoping for the promotion.

The girl cop stepped forward and said, "I cuffed him; I'll let him go." I liked her for that. The detective nodded at my wrists.

His name was Bill Gubman, and he was in charge of the Ahmed Hassan killing. He was also my closest friend. We'd gone through the Academy together, stood side by side at graduation, become rookies in the same police district. We'd stayed friends when I started smoking half of what I confiscated on the street. He'd covered for me even though he had ambitions that were bigger than mine and covering for me could wreck every dream of success he ever smiled at in the middle of the night. He'd stuck by me all the way, till I crashed my cruiser into a newsstand, stoned silly, blood alcohol .34, high enough to kill some men. After that, we didn't talk to each other for a couple years, until he called, middle of the night, asking me to set up an appointment for his wife, Eileen, with the substance-abuse counselor who'd helped me with my habits. Then, Bill understood.

Now, he was the top homicide detective in the Eighteenth District, and I was a PI rubbing my wrists where the girl cop's matching steel bracelets had chafed.

For the next hour and a half, the police looked for evidence. There wasn't much. They pried the bullet out of the door frame and put it in an evidence bag for analysis. They dusted for prints. They found a security camera—broken—on a shelf in the supply room. They carefully reconstructed the killing, but the event line was pretty obvious. Ahmed Hassan had taken two bullets, one in the neck, the other in the chest. Neither shot at close range. He'd dragged himself twelve feet along a glass case. He'd fallen through the case to the floor. The medical examiner spent ten minutes with the corpse and cleared it for the morgue.

I told my story twice to different officers: I was in my car, waiting for the deliveryman to finish his delivery. He carried four boxes into the store, three on a dolly, one on his shoulder. I heard three gunshots. The deliveryman ran outside and drove away in his white van. Sorry, no license plate number. I went into the store and found Ahmed Hassan dying. The back door was open and three of the boxes and the dolly were gone. The fourth box was on the floor. End of story.

The second officer hammered at me for an ID of the deliveryman.

"It was dark," I said.

"Any distinguishing marks?"

"He was thirty-five or forty feet from my car. I wasn't paying attention to him. He was just a guy in a yellow hat."

"A guy in a yellow hat?"

"That's right."

He shook his head, frustrated. "And what did the guy who went out the back look like?"

"Curious George."

"This is very important," the cop said.

"I didn't see a guy in the back."

"Who shot the store owner? The deliveryman or someone else?"

"How do I know?" I said, but I figured the deliveryman had shot him, since there was a slug in the storage room's door frame and the angle was right for him to have shot it. But someone else had been in the store. No question about it. Someone had stood by the storage room and scared the deliveryman plenty. The deliveryman had dropped his boxes, shot, and then run from the store when he was done shooting. The missing boxes interested me. Whoever else had been in the store must have taken them. The boxes interested Bill Gubman, too. Four of them had come in the front door and three had gone out the back, all in about one minute. In that minute, Ahmed Hassan had gotten shot. Four hundred dollars and change in the cash register said whoever had stolen the boxes wasn't after money.

Bill looked through the one box that remained. I already knew what was inside: DVDs with short titles that someone tried to make playful—*Fit to Be Tied*, *Whipped Cream*—that kind of thing. Mostly boy-boy, if you believed the pictures on the packages. A packing slip said a company called BlackLite Productions made the DVDs, but there was no address or contact information.

I leaned against a wall and tried to think of reasons why someone would kill for a few boxes of porn. From the look on Bill's face as he thumbed through the DVDs, he had no idea why, either.

After a while, the boy cop wandered over. He may have been short and skinny, but he puffed up his chest, and who knows, there might be more to him than it looked like. He stared me in the eyes and said, "Sorry for earlier. I overreacted."

His name tag said he was Stan Jersyk. "You did all right," I said. "Better than getting yourself shot."

He nodded, as if he already knew it.

After Bill got his fill of the DVDs, he wandered over, too. "You all right?"

"Fresh from the bakery," I said.

He shrugged. "You look like shit." He smiled.

"I'm tired of this, Bill," I said.

"Yeah," he said, like he was tired, too, and no amount of sleep would help. "Go home."

I didn't like the party, so I let him show me to the door.

The September night was hot, the air still. Clusters of men, most in pajamas or bathrobes, hung out in the doorways of the nearby buildings, feeding on the electricity of crime. Two young uniformed cops stood behind the yellow police ribbon, keeping the curious back. The cops wore bored faces, but with a murder twenty feet behind them, you could tell they felt the electricity, too. Four news vans were on the curb across the street. Their lamps lighted up the night like sunshine. A couple reporters talked on-camera. Another looked in a mirror and drew lipstick onto her lips. One more leaned against a van, smoking a cigarette, looking like he wished he was in bed. As soon as they saw me, they ran across the street, dragging cameramen behind them.

The reporter with the lipstick managed to get to me first. "Are you the officer in charge?" she asked.

I ducked under the ribbon and came out next to her. She was small and thin and had a great mouth, but too much lipstick. Red lipstick. And I'd seen enough red for one night. Her eyes were green and too alive for the middle of the night. She'd gelled her hair out on both sides of her head like blond turtle shells. She wore a matching navy blue skirt and jacket and had unbuttoned the jacket to show a little bit of breast. She was pretty, but there was too much of her.

"Run the tape," she said to the cameraman, and then to me again: "Are you the officer in charge?"

The camera was running and the two uniformed cops stood out of earshot. "Yes, I am."

"Can you tell us what happened?"

"Well," I said, "a man got killed."

"How was he killed?" She made her question sound like the answer would make a difference.

"Dead is dead; it doesn't matter how you get there."

"Shot?" she asked. Like television viewers needed this information before they could return to their normal lives.

I looked in her bright green eyes. "Shot twice." I touched my finger softly to her neck and let it linger, feeling her heat and fear. "Shot here," I said. I moved my finger to her left breast. "And here."

She frowned. "Thank you."

She turned to the camera, but I added, "He fell through a display case." I pointed at her eyes. "Glass shards in the eyes. He died blind."

More frowning, and another "Thank you," but she didn't sound like she meant it. She forced a smile at the camera and said, "Live from North Dearborn, this is Deborah Hughes." The camera light went off and she spun toward me. "You bastard. What the hell was that!" She wiped her neck as if I'd put a cockroach on it.

I gave her calm. "Don't ask what you don't want to know."

I walked across the street and got in my car. It was a green 1989 Skylark, half rust, with 180,000 miles on it and too little tread on the tires. In the close heat of the September night, the smells of all the years I'd driven that car hung in the air. Right then, the car felt like the nicest place in the world.

I put my gun in the glove compartment, then took Ahmed Hassan's court summons from the passenger seat and ripped it into pieces. His kids would need to figure out how to eat without him.

THREE

NIGHTS LIKE THIS, I didn't drag the dirt of my life into my home. Nights like this, if I couldn't sleep, I drove down Lincoln Avenue and looked for a woman who could help me forget myself for an hour or two, or else I parked by the lake and listened to the waves breaking on the sand. *Hush*, the waves said, *hush*. The deep lake sang me a lullaby. Sometimes that was enough to make me forget, too. If I figured I could sleep, I would go to my office on South Wabash and use the sagging couch for a bed.

I drove south through the city to the office. Except for maintenance and housekeeping workers who ghosted past lighted windows, the buildings on my block at 1:30 on a Monday night were empty. The street and sidewalk were empty, too. I parked under the El tracks outside my building as a train jolted and screeched past.

My office was on the eighth floor of an eight-story building, the only office on the top floor. The rest of the floor was occupied by a secretarial school where they taught inner-city kids who'd gotten federal grants for vocational training. A woman named Roselle Turner ran the school for maximum profit and gave the students as little as she could before sending them back to the streets, usually with no jobs. Still, no matter what she did to keep them down, someone could learn something in a place like this. I wondered why I never did.

A steel plate at eye level on my office door said JOE KOZMARSKI. PRIVATE INVESTIGATION AND DETECTIVE SERVICES. My office had everything I needed: a gray metal desk, a computer, four file cabinets, a couch, and a window facing east over the El tracks into an insurance building. I left the lights off, stripped off my clothes, and made the couch into a bed.

Then I went to the window and looked out. In daylight or under a full moon, a sliver of Lake Michigan showed through a gap between the insurance building and the building to the north of it. But now the sky was dark. I opened the window enough to let the warm city air blow in. Another El train jolted past on the steel tracks. I breathed deep, felt fatigue rise through my bones. My office clock said the time was 1:41. I climbed onto the couch and watched the clock numbers change. I had a vial of Ambien in a desk drawer, but tonight it could sleep alone. The clock said 1:42, then 1:43. The last I saw, it was 1:48.

I dreamed of the boy again. He was sleeping on the kitchen floor—calm, the way only a sleeping child looks calm. Except one leg was twisted back from the knee, like a broken plastic spoon. His mother, the one I was watching in a custody case, sat at the kitchen table eating scrambled eggs and drinking coffee. I stood at the door to the hallway. I had let myself in when no one answered the door. "What's wrong with Kevin?" I asked. Kevin's mother didn't answer. She lifted a forkful of eggs to her mouth and chased it with a sip of coffee. Then she replied, "He's dead." She ate another bite of eggs. Calm. My head spun. I sat on the floor to keep from falling. "Dead?" Kevin's father had hired me to make sure his son was okay. His son was not okay. Kevin's mother nodded. "He's dead." More coffee. I crawled to the boy. I smoothed the hair off his forehead with my hand. His forehead was as cold as the floor. I recoiled, then crept close again. I tried to lift him in my arms but couldn't. He weighed a thousand pounds. I had never tried to lift a thing so heavy.

Sometime during the night, a wind rose. It cut through my dream. It was the kind of wind that brings September storms to Chicago, building from the northeast and tumbling down Lake Michigan. The lake water turns the color of slate. The trees bend like they'll break. The air cools, the sky turns gray, and summer suddenly seems a long time ago.

I pulled the sheet around me but shook with cold in my sleep and woke early. A couple minutes before six, I got up, still wrapped in the sheet, and looked out the window at the chilly morning sky. I shook again, from the cold, from Ahmed Hassan's murder last night, from Kevin Morales's death on a summer day three years ago.

But now, outside the window, the world looked changed. Nothing of the hot night of murder remained. Through the crack between the buildings across the street, Lake Michigan glowed in the early light. White-caps crawled across the surface as far as the eye could see. A plastic shopping bag danced in the draft outside my window, then rose and disappeared over the building top, and suddenly I felt lighter than I'd felt in months, like I could rise, too, above all that was holding me down. Ahmed Hassan died on a hot night, and now a northern wind chilled the morning, and Hassan would never shiver in it. Kevin Morales wouldn't, either.

I didn't want to think about all that had been holding me down this morning. I didn't want to be truthful. I wanted to keep looking out the window. I knew what the half-light in the office behind me would show: my desk, the pictures on the walls, the certificates next to my desk, my clothes piled on the floor, my gun on top of the clothes, all the stuff that reminded me of death—Kevin Morales's, Ahmed Hassan's, my own sooner or later. I wanted to rise above all that in the crisp early-fall air.

In one of the file drawers, there were shorts and a pair of running shoes. I put them on. No T-shirt.

I ran north on Wabash, under the El tracks, in the dim light. The cold air bit at me, made me run faster. By the time I got to Adams Street, I started to warm up. I zigzagged north and east to Grant Park and then the harbor. The water was almost black. Sailboats bounced on their moorings in the harbor chop. Halyards rang off aluminum masts like bells for the dead I had known.

The asphalt jogging path traced the artificial shore-line, landfill dumped in the 1930s so the city could pour an eight-lane highway, and now as solid as anything else in town. Developers had sunk dozens of luxury high rises into the shaky soil, and none of them had fallen yet. Good for the developers. Good for the people who gazed down on the bouncing sailboats from their luxury high-rise windows. They'd learned something, done something. For three miles, I ran, face into the northeast wind, then turned and started back, wind pushing me from behind. At Randolph Street, the path turned uphill into the Grant Park gardens. I ran until I got to Buckingham Fountain. Six bronze sea dragons spat fat streams of water into the air. The sea dragons had giant horse heads and big flat saucer eyes that were as blank as the eyes of Ahmed Hassan. Their fat bodies snaked out behind them. There was pain in them, the pain of being hated and hunted. They had no marks on their copper skin, but I knew they were wounded. You don't twist like a snake and vomit water thirty feet in the air unless you're wounded.

Their problem, not mine, I thought, and I jogged back toward my office. By the time I got to Grandma's Kitchen a half block away, I was hungry and felt almost like one of the living again.

Almost every day when I was working at my office, I ate breakfast or lunch at Grandma's. One old wait-ress who worked weekends probably was someone's grandma, but three Greek brothers owned the place, and they cooked, took orders, and worked the cash register. The place smelled like hamburger grease even at seven o'clock in the morning. But they made a good fried egg.

Alexandros, the oldest brother, rang up my order on the cash register. Behind him on the wall was a picture of him with his wife and three kids. He wore a white sleeveless T-shirt in the picture; he wore a white sleeveless T-shirt at the cash register; he always wore a white sleeveless T-shirt. Next to his picture were pictures of the other brothers with their wives and kids. They wore white T-shirts, too. It was a family place.

He looked at me sweating in my shorts as if he was concerned. "You put a shirt on, Joe, or you get sick," he said. At least he sounded like a grandma. He ran his fingers through a tuft of hair on his shoulder. "Or you need to grow more of this. It keeps you warm on winter nights. Or"—he winked—"you need a woman to keep you warm."

"I'll take the woman," I said.

"You know, I got a cousin—"

I laughed. "I'll get back to you about your cousin." I picked up my take-out breakfast and went to the door.

Alexandros laughed, too. "I think she like you."

Roselle Turner was waiting for the elevator when I walked back into my building. We said good morning. She was a small woman, mid-forties, with dark eyes and black hair streaked with gray. She stared at me as if I were a piece of bacon.

Suddenly, everyone thought I was sexy. Maybe my change of mood showed. Or maybe no one was used to seeing me half-naked in the city on a cold September morning.

When the elevator came, Roselle blinked and raised her eyes from my chest. We got on alone, and she stood close to me. At the fourth floor, she said, "Do you know who you look like?"

My ex-wife, Corrine, used to say I looked like Lech Walesa in the Solidarity days, but with abs and forget the mustache. "Who?" I said.

Her smile got coy. "I can't decide. A little Robert De Niro and a lot of Bill Murray."

"Bill Murray?"

She nodded. "When he had more hair."

"Okay, a hairy Bill Murray."

She looked me up and down. "But taller, of course."

"Of course."

A bell rang at the eighth floor. She wrinkled her nose in a way that someone must have told her was cute. "And you've got nice abs." She got off in front of me and put some hip in her walk.

That decided it: In my next life, I would be a secretary. I would type correspondence for Roselle Turner, punching out fifteen words a minute.

FOUR

WHEN I WALKED BACK into my office a couple minutes after seven, the red light on my answering machine was blinking. Larry Weiss had probably gotten the news about his client's ex taking two bullets. Undoubtedly, he wanted to know what I'd done to screw up his percentage of the child-support payments. I ignored the machine and changed into jeans and a white sweatshirt, then pulled my desk chair over to the window. I ate breakfast watching the gray clouds sail south over the building tops. South seemed like a good direction to go. I figured if I had any sense, I would close my business, sell my house, and move to Florida, fish until my money ran out, then take a job to earn some cash and fish some more. I would live easy. No more dead men lying in piles of glass. No more bad dreams.

When I finished my eggs, I looked out my window some more and daydreamed about fishing for grouper off the Florida coast. Around eight o'clock, I got up and punched the play button on the answering machine. The voice on the recording shook me out of my happy dream. "Hey, Joe. It's Peter Rifkin. Saw you on TV this morning. Give me a call when you get a chance." He left a phone number and hung up.

My stomach dropped at the name Peter Rifkin. Judge Rifkin. He'd been best friends with my dad and once had been like a second father to me. I hadn't talked with him in fifteen years and didn't want to talk to him now. But you didn't ignore the judge, even if he was no longer a judge and even if he was responsible for your dad's death. I dialed the number he'd left on my machine. After three rings, he answered. "Rifkin."

"Hello, Judge," I said.

"Joe!" I could feel him grin over the telephone line. "How're you doing?"

"Not so hot. You saw the TV interview."

"Yeah, that was ugly. But it was good to see you again. I'm watching the morning news—I've got time to do that now—and who comes on but Joey Kozmarski." No one but the judge called me Joey, even when I was a kid. "I think, What's he doing, impersonating an officer? I hear about you time to time, but it's a long time since I've seen your face. And then there you are on the morning news. And I say, Jesus Christ, I know that boy; I've got to give him a call and say 'Good work.'"

"Good work in getting involved in a shopkeeper's murder, or in worrying the reporter who talked to me?"

"Whatever."

"How'd you find my phone number?"

"You're in the phone book, aren't you?" He sounded insulted.

"You looked me up in the phone book?"

"No," he said, "I got your number from Larry Weiss." Larry. Maybe giving my number to the judge was payback for my letting his client's ex get killed. "He told me about you and Corrine splitting. Sorry to hear about that. You doing okay?"

"Yeah," I said, lying. "We both wanted it this way. Where are you living now, Judge?"

"Beverly Shores, down in the Indiana Dunes. An hour from the city."

"Fifteen years ago, I would've figured the only way anyone would ever get you to leave Chicago was by convicting you and sending you downstate. What are you doing in the Dunes?"

"Taking it easy, mostly. I bought a nice big house in the woods. I'm in semiretirement. After they kicked me off the bench, I started a business cutting grass on highway median strips. Big state and federal contracts, you know, and cheap labor: Mexican and Dominican. Except for the bidding, it's six-months-a-year work. Other half is vacation. Even in season, I walk the beach every morning looking for driftwood." Another guy who'd learned from his mistakes, though if the judge was in it, it had to have a dirty angle, especially if it involved government bids. "Life is good," he said. "But you should come see me. I've got a friend who would like to talk to you today if you could use the work."

"I could use a couple weeks walking the beach looking for driftwood," I said.

"This friend's an old friend of yours, too."

"Who's that?"

"I'll take you fishing while you're here. The way we used to. Me and you and . . ." He paused.

"My dad?"

"That's right. Me and you and your dad."

"I'm not licensed to work in Indiana. Not licensed to fish, either."

"Yeah, I know. But the trout don't know, and they're biting like mosquitoes right now."

I looked out the window. Clouds were barreling across the sky. "This storm's got to be pushing eight-foot waves your way."

"The wind's almost blown out," he said. "Trust me. By this afternoon, we'll just have some swells."

"I'm going to pass on this one, Judge."

"I'll pay you fifteen thousand up front."

"I usually charge fifteen hundred."

"I know. Larry Weiss told me. But this time, you'll charge fifteen grand."

I didn't want to see the judge. We'd hurt each other too many times already. But fifteen thousand would pay for a lot of Band-Aids and a lot of roses for Dad's cemetery plot. Besides, I was curious what would be worth that kind of cash to the judge.

"I'll be there a little before eleven," I said.

When we hung up, I stared at the window and wondered what the hell I was doing. I figured it was easier to blame someone else, so I dialed Larry Weiss. Except for when he was playing poker, which he would do all night, he was a lazy guy. He stayed in bed till 9:30 or 10:00 unless he had a court appointment. He never scheduled a meeting before noon. He was a smart guy and did his best to ignore his potential.

When his wife handed him the phone, he shouted, "What the hell happened last night?"

"Why the hell did you give the judge my number?" I asked.

He paused. "I'm sorry, Joe. The judge woke me up this morning. I wasn't thinking."

"Yeah, that's okay. Sorry about Hassan."

"What the fuck. It happens. You all right?"

"Yeah, I'm fine. I'm good. No one shot me. The shooter put a couple holes in your bankroll, though."

"That's what I hear. I also hear you got a good look at the guy."

"The shooter? Nah, I barely saw him. He was just a guy in the dark across the street. No one to me."

"Cop I talked to seems to think you ID'd him."

"Cops can think what they want."

"Oh well, it's done. Hassan was a little bankroll, a couple bills and some change. I'll make it back playing cards. Why'd the judge want to talk to you?"

"He wants to take me fishing."

"Really?"

"And he's got a job for me."

Larry whistled. "You go to work for the judge, you be careful," he said.

"That was fifteen years ago. He's an old man now."

"I don't care if he's buried six feet under, he's still trouble."

"I don't worry about trouble," I said. "That's why I've got you."

We hung up, and I went to the men's room I share with the secretarial school. I stripped off my sweat-shirt, shaved, and pretended one of the sinks was a shower. Then I went back to my office and called Mom.

I did my best imitation of a cheerful son. "Good morning, Mom."

"You're on TV this morning, Joe," she answered. She said it like the news was showing my mug shot. "What were you doing there? Why were you in that place?"

"I was working," I said, calm. "It's not like I killed the man."

"No, you didn't kill him, but he's dead, isn't he?"

"Yes, he is."

"What are you doing today?" she asked.

"I'm going fishing." I didn't tell her I was going to see the judge. That was something she never needed to know. "Why?"

"I want you to come over."

"I'll be out all day, Mom."

"You're out all day, then I'll cook dinner. Come at six. I've got a surprise for you."

"Does it involve Sophy?" Sophy was Mom's sister, visiting from Miami with her eleven-year-old grandson, Jason. Since she'd arrived two weeks ago, I'd eaten enough pierogi with her to hibernate in a snowdrift till spring. If the surprise involved her, I didn't want it.

"Sophy left yesterday."

"All right, Mom," I said. "Six."

"I love you."

"You, too, Mom."

"Be careful fishing," she said, like she knew something about the dangers of hooks and worms.

Jeans and a sweatshirt were good enough for a day in the Indiana Dunes. I strapped on my over-the-shoulder rig and holstered my Glock 23, slipped on a gray jacket. That was good enough for the Dunes, too. "Be careful fishing," Mom had said. If a rainbow trout attacked me, I would know what to do. If the judge acted up, same thing.

FIVE

THE JUDGE LIVED IN a big two-story Cape built into the dunes, with a three-car garage and a swimming pool. The place would be called a mansion anywhere else. Here it was a beach house. The judge said he swam in the pool every morning until the first frost. If you stood on the diving board, you could see Lake Michigan.

The judge cooked burgers on the patio grill. He was a small man, seventy-two years old, and had a gut. But he still had sparkling blue eyes and perfect little teeth. Carla Pakorian, a woman I'd never met before, stood next to him. She was in her mid-thirties and had the healthy look of someone who'd grown up hiking in the Dunes. Sturdy legs and shoulders, a wide face, and a quick laugh. She slipped her hand in and out of the judge's, but she kept her eyes on Bob Piedras. Bob worked for the judge's company, purchasing equipment and managing the cheap labor. When I was growing up, he lived down the block from me—and the judge—on the northwest side of Chicago. He was the old friend the judge had promised. Like me, he was forty-three years old, but he looked twenty-eight. His mom was a Polish Jew, his dad a Mexican Catholic, and he'd gotten the best of them both. He was tall and had olive skin, blond hair, and jade green eyes. Carla Pakorian wasn't the first woman to stare at him while holding hands with another man.

It didn't matter to the judge where Carla Pakorian was staring, though. He had his eyes on her. When I arrived, he introduced her as the Realtor who sold him the house and then became his girlfriend.

She laughed at the girlfriend comment. "Yeah, right, old man."

"What?" the judge asked. "Can't old men like beautiful women?"

Carla said, "Isn't he charming?" sounding like she meant it. She even took her eyes off Bob for a moment.

In the living room, the judge tossed down a hamburger and a beer, then sprang around, getting drinks and food for everyone. "You should have seen Joey on TV this morning," he said to Bob and Carla. "He looked half crazy. Jesus! I thought the reporter would wet her pants. Probably thought Joey was the killer."

Carla said, "The producers must have loved that. Real fear."

The judge turned to me. "You know, you could get in trouble saying you're the officer in charge. A guy like you: kicked off the force, then wandering around saying you're a cop on live television. Looks like you're trying to compensate."

I nodded. "They cut the footage that showed me driving away with my siren on."

Carla smiled. "Why'd they kick you off the force?"

"Got drunk one night and wiped out a newsstand with my cruiser."

Her mouth formed an *O*. She had nice lips, nice teeth.

"It was three in the morning. No one got hurt," I said. "I blew through a couple thousand dollars in magazines, though."

The judge cracked a smile. "Who's really heading the murder investigation?"

"Bill Gubman," I said.

"Gubman? Jesus Christ! It's a family reunion. You should've called me, and I would've come over with the barbecue grill." He told Carla, "Back a lot of years ago, Joey's dad and I were best friends. Used to go fishing together. Sometimes Joey went with us, sometimes other kids, like Bob, from the neighborhood. When Joey became a cop, he got to be friends with Gubman, and he sometimes fished with us, too."

He didn't mention that our happy little family broke apart when he got indicted for bribery and left the neighborhood. And he didn't mention how he worked a plea agreement by agreeing to name names or how my dad died a month after he got his hands on records that showed the judge had falsely accused him of passing him a bribe. I guess I didn't expect the judge to mention those things.

"So, did you ID the killer for Gubman?" he asked.

"Nah," I admitted for the tenth time. "I barely noticed

him going into the store, and he was just a panicking guy when he ran back out."

The judge laughed. For him, Ahmed Hassan's killing was just a good story, a way to pass a September day in the Dunes. His laugh made me feel sick. I said to Bob, "I hear you need a detective. What kind of trouble you in?"

He looked nervously at the judge, and the judge said, "Let's talk about that on the water."

Carla carried her dishes into the kitchen. The judge tilted his head and watched her go.

"Why did you invite her?" Bob asked. "She doesn't need to know about this."

"She's good company," the judge said.

Bob gave him a look. "Yeah, and you're an old man."

The judge smirked. "What's that got to do with the shape of her ass?" So much for charm. He turned to me. "Bobby has screwed everything he could put his hands on for the last twenty-five years. Somehow—don't ask me how—he doesn't have AIDS and doesn't have warts. They'd make him a saint for that miracle if he wasn't half Jewish. And then he questions *my* sex life."

"What am I doing here, judge?" I said.

He gave a charming grin. "Going fishing."

THE JUDGE KEPT A 280 Sun Sport in a slip at the Washington Park Marina, about half an hour from his house. When we got out of his Suburban in the marina parking lot, spray blew from the harbor and slapped our cheeks. The wind whistled through the halyards.

The judged yelled against the wind. "We'll catch our limit. Trust me."

"Not a chance," I said.

The harbor was all choppy waves, and under the waves a big rolling swell lifted the floating docks and set them down like something huge and breathing. We walked out to the judge's slip. If you stood his boat on its end, you could use it as a rocket. Twenty-nine feet of speed and power. We untied and motored toward the harbor mouth. Eight-foot waves crashed against the breakwater and roared through the gap.

"No way," shouted Carla Pakorian.

The judge gunned the motor toward the mouth. "No?" He glanced at Bob. "What do you think?"

Bob shook his head no.

The judge looked disgusted. He cut the gas a little. "How about you, Joe? You going to let a little weather stop you from catching a fish?" He stared at me hard, daring me to call his bluff.

"Fish don't bite in weather like this."

He held the stare, then grinned and turned the steering wheel. "Okay, nonbelievers," he said. The boat rode the chop back through the harbor, past the judge's slip, all the way to the far end, where unused mooring cans hung in water calmed by a windbreak of trees. The judge had Bob tie a line to the can closest to the wall, and then he cut the engine and pulled fishing rods and a gallon carton of live minnows out of the side storage. He rigged up a hook, minnow, and sinker for each of us, then told us to cast toward the trees.

When my hook touched the water, a fish hit it. I reeled

in a pound-and-a-half yellow perch. In less than five minutes, all the men had caught one, Carla two. After fifteen minutes, I had four. "What's the limit on perch?" I asked.

The judge grinned, as if he could magically produce fish whenever and wherever he wanted. "Who the hell knows? Fifteen, I think."

I grinned back at him. "Four's enough for me."

"On the way back to my house, we'll troll for salmon out of the windows of my Suburban."

I tried to hand him the fishing pole, but he refused to take it. "Only after you say 'You are the king of fishermen. I trust you, Judge Rifkin.'"

"No." I put the pole down in the boat and made myself comfortable on the vinyl seat. "You impress me. You always did. But I'll never trust you again."

"Do you believe this guy?" the judge said, still grinning.

"What's this about?" I said. "Why did you invite me here?"

He shrugged. "Do you want me to tell him, Bobby?"

"Go ahead," Bob said.

The judge put his own pole and mine back in the side storage. Bob took his line out of the water and listened. Only Carla kept fishing. "Three weeks ago, did you hear about that Vietnamese girl who died after a night out partying?" the judge asked.

"I think I saw something on the news," I said. "They found the body at a hotel by the airport."

"The O'Hare Hilton," he said. "Her name was Le Thi Hanh. Her friends called her 'Hannah.' She was drinking at a nightclub called Club Nine, and she met a man and a woman. She left with them. Next morning, a hotel maid found her in the closet with her throat cut."

"Why are you worried about this?"

"A couple reasons," the judge said. "The small one is I own a piece of Club Nine. One of my fun investments. Keeps me in the game."

"You worried about liability?"

"That's part of it. Looks like she was high. If she got the drugs at the club, there's a lawsuit, and I practiced law enough years on both sides of the bench to know I would lose."

"What's the big reason?"

"Bobby here was Hannah's boyfriend."

"Sorry to hear that," I said.

Bob looked shaken. "Thanks," he mumbled, so softly, I hardly could hear him. I couldn't hear him.

"It's ugly," said the judge. "But it gets worse. The cops think Bobby did it. They haven't named him as a suspect, but word is they'll arrest him by the end of the week."

"What about the couple Hannah left the club with?"

"Same couple she went to the Hilton with. Security camera shows that. But the cops don't think the couple did it. Hannah had her clothes on. No sexual assault. No evidence of sex at all. And there would have been if the couple had killed her for a thrill. Makes better sense to the cops that Hannah's jealous boyfriend followed her and the couple into the Hilton and killed her. Then the couple got scared and ran, checked out in the middle of the night. Security camera shows them leaving, too, heading into the airport."

I turned to Bob. "Does it show you going into the ho-tel?"

"No," he said, pale, like the thought sickened him.

The judge said, "But it wouldn't necessarily. There're four entrances. Only the one by the front desk has a camera."

"Who's the couple?"

The judge shook his head. "They paid cash. Used fake IDs, false names. So far, no one's traced them."

"That kind of makes them look guilty, doesn't it?" Carla said.

"It doesn't mean much," I told her. "A couple goes out to score a threesome, they might not want to use their real names. It's not like they'll identify them-selves now when every news station in the country would be happy to show their photos." I turned to Bob. "Any other reason you're a suspect?"

He looked away. "I got arrested awhile back with an-other girlfriend. But the charges were dropped."

The judge laughed. "The girl was high-maintenance. They argued."

"You hit her?" I asked.

"Not hard," Bob said.

"We used to call that passion," the judge said.

"Who are 'we'?" Carla said.

"Did you kill Hannah?" I asked.

"No." Bob shook his head. "No."

"Okay. Who's your lawyer?"

"The judge got Donald Sanke for me."

"Good for you," I said. Donald Sanke was the best criminal defense attorney in Chicago.

I asked the judge, "Why do you want to hire me when you've got Sanke and his people on this?"

The judge shrugged. "So far, Sanke's people haven't turned up anything that's going to save Bob. I don't think they'll get serious until the police charge Bob. When you're Donald Sanke, you prioritize, and right now Bob isn't a priority. By the time he becomes one, it might be too late. I know you've had your problems, Joe, but I also know your work is good. And even if it's been awhile, you know Bob, and you know what he's capable of, and it's not this, not killing a girl."

"Tell me about Hannah," I said to Bob.

"She was a party girl," he said. "She took classes at the Art Institute, but mostly she hung out at clubs, especially Club Nine. She worked as a cocktail waitress sometimes."

"She from Chicago?"

"She grew up on Kenmore, in Little Vietnam."

"Family still there?"

"Her mom and dad are, and two younger brothers. They own a grocery store called Nam Hai. She's also got an older brother who's an estate lawyer. He's the only one she was talking to. The rest of the family was upset with her for moving out of the neighborhood, partying so much, dating someone like me."

"Half Mexican *and* half Jew," said the judge. "There's got to be a limit to tolerance."

"What about the night she died?" I asked.

"I went to her apartment at ten," Bob said. "We drank some vodka, and she did a hit of ecstasy. Then we went to Club Nine. After an hour or so, she started dancing with the couple. I saw them leaving, and I tried to stop her. We argued, but she left anyway."

"If her killer was someone she knew, who would it be?" I asked him.

He shook his head, looking sad and tired. "I don't know. I've thought about it, but no one, really. I mean, I met the older brother. Seems like a nice guy. Lives downtown on the Gold Coast, though he's in Thailand right now. I don't know about the rest of the family. I just know that for them she was the bad girl and they were ashamed of her."

"Who else?"

"She's got her friends at the Art Institute. And before me, she went out with one of her teachers. I know he wasn't happy when she broke it off. A guy named Charlie Morell."

The judge interrupted again. "I'll pay your fees. You want the job?"

"Why did you need to take me fishing to tell me all this?"

The judge laughed. "I thought you'd like it. Like the old days. Me and you and your dad."

"The old days are gone, Judge," I said.

"I know they are. I know it. But—" He didn't finish the sentence. He probably knew there was no way to finish it that wouldn't make him sound like a jerk.

SIX

I DROVE BACK TO the city a little after four o'clock. A folder sat on the passenger seat with information on Le Thi Hanh, including her parents' address in Little Vietnam, and a check from the judge made out to me for fifteen thousand dollars. Bob had come up with two pictures of Hannah. One was recent and showed a thin, short-haired Vietnamese woman with a smile that curled up higher on the right than on the left, like she was thinking wicked thoughts. She wore a little skirt and a low-cut shirt that showed plenty. The other was older, probably a high school yearbook picture. She had longer hair, a prim smile, and a white blouse buttoned up at the neck.

Just the night before, I'd had a picture of Ahmed Hassan on the passenger seat. I figured I should hang a sign from the headrest: RESERVED FOR THE DEAD.

My visit to the judge didn't make a lot of sense. Priority or no priority, Donald Sanke had the resources to turn the city upside down and shake it until proof of Bob's innocence fell out of its pockets. Me? I had a Glock 23, an old Buick Skylark, and an office computer. If my own life depended on it, I would fire me and hire Sanke.

Maybe the judge saw this as a chance to make up with me for his two betrayals. The first came in 1980, when the FBI stung the Cook County court system, nailing every judge they could put their fingers on for taking bribes. Over the next eight years, they got Rifkin and fourteen other judges, forty-six lawyers, four court clerks, and eighteen cops and deputy sheriffs. They didn't convict Dad, but after the judge's accusation, the FBI investigated him, and that investigation stopped his career. It put a stain on Dad that never went away, no matter how clean a life he lived. Everyone thought he'd pissed on himself. And no one promotes a guy who's pissed on himself.

Dad was innocent, and he figured the FBI investigation of him was a simple mistake. It had happened to other cops he knew, and he knew his friendship with the judge made him look suspicious. So he lived with it. He went to work every day knowing that his bosses thought he'd pissed on himself, knowing he would never become a district captain himself. He stayed best friends with the judge even after the judge's guilty plea, because, for him, friends stayed friends. But then he wised up and used the Freedom of Information Act, got his hands on some records that the FBI let slip into the public domain without blacking out the names. He learned that the judge himself had accused him of passing bribes.

But in the years between the judge's accusation and Dad's discovery of the accusation, the judge had acted as loyal as a Saint Bernard. When Dad had a heart attack scare, the judge had driven him and Mom to the hospital and then slept in the waiting room for two days while they ran tests. Dad and the judge had spent more time together than when the judge was still on the bench. Afterward, it seemed like the judge had been trying for years to work off his guilt for hurting Dad. A ten-year apology.

So, as bad as that betrayal was, I could forgive him for it. But I couldn't forgive him for one that came later.

Now, though, I had his check on the seat next to me. It was dirty money. The judge was dirty. I wondered if I was dirty, too.

I made a mental note to think more about that later. Then I thought about the people I needed to talk to about Le Thi Hanh: her neighbors at her apartment building, her family in Little Vietnam, her brother the estate lawyer, the teacher she'd dated at the Art Institute, her Art Institute friends, club hoppers at Club 9, the front-desk people at the O'Hare Hilton, the maid who'd found the body, anyone else along the way who had known her. If Bob was right, the Art Institute teacher and Hannah's family were the most important people on my list, but talking to them would take time. I had less than two hours before I needed to be at Mom's house for dinner and the surprise.

So I headed to Club 9, which was in an old two-story brick theater on Sheffield, just north of the Belmont

El station. A white marquee advertised a band called Modest Mouse. A punked-out girl crouched against the brick wall by the entrance. She wore a black T-shirt with pink lettering. It said KEEP STARING. I MIGHT DO A TRICK. I started into the club, then stopped. "What kind of trick?"

"Shoot Ping-Pong balls from my butt," she said.

Inside, the place looked like a burned-out firehouse. Black walls rose from a black floor high into black metal beams and ceiling tiles. Five chrome fire poles, scattered around the room, reached ten feet into the air, then up through platforms into empty cages, where hired dancers could prance around like nervous zoo animals. Heavy-metal music blasted out of speakers.

A bar with a long row of stools ran along the left side of the room. A man sat on one of the stools, playing solitaire. He didn't seem to notice me behind him. A bottle of Sierra Nevada pale ale stood on the counter by the cards, two empties next to it. He had on black jeans, black boots, and a red short-sleeved T-shirt. A tattoo of a woman on a motorcycle rode across his right bicep. She had long hair, big naked breasts, short shorts, and knee-high boots. He must've driven on different highways than I did. His hair and beard were somewhere between brown and red and tangled thick as a scrub pad. He peeled a queen of diamonds off his deck of cards and placed it on a king of clubs.

I tapped his shoulder, and he turned as if expecting me. He gave me a thumbs-up, then ran around to the back of the bar and turned a knob. The music cut off. "Hey," he said, "you with Modest Mouse?"

"I'm Modest Mouse's brother, Proud Possum."

He reached for the volume knob again.

"Give me a minute," I said.

"Who the fuck are you?" he asked.

The wall behind the bar was covered with hundreds of stickers naming the bands that had played in the club: the Demons, False Hope, Big Sister, Magenta Placenta, and dozens more like that. Nothing better than Proud Possum. I gave him a business card and told him I was looking into the death of Le Thi Hanh.

"Hannah," he said, and his eyes glazed over sad. "You want a drink?"

I eyed the bottle of Jack Daniel's across the bar. "A Coke, thanks."

He poured the Coke. "Who are you working for?"

"One of the club owners, Peter Rifkin."

"The judge?" he asked with a tired smile, like he also knew the judge was dirty. "Yeah, him and Hannah were tight."

"The judge? I thought Bob Piedras dated her."

"Not tight like that. They were just real friendly. She liked to hang around drinking, and the judge liked to buy her drinks."

"Sounds like she got the better end of it."

"I think the judge figured she was broke, but it turns out she had a nice apartment downtown and drove a BMW."

"Was she Bob Piedras's girlfriend?"

He shook his head. "She wasn't anyone's girlfriend. She slept with him, if that's what you mean, but she slept with a lot of other guys, too. Lately, she was mostly with

Bob, though, yeah. You know, Bob always has a party around him, and she liked to party; she liked to have fun." His voice had admiration, like partying and having fun were worth fighting and dying for.

"Who were her other friends?"

"She sometimes came in with a girl called Jamie. Don't know her last name. She shares a house with a bunch of party kids in Rogers Park. They all hung together. Hannah, too."

"She was with Bob the night she got killed?"

He reached across the bar and got his beer, took a long drink. "They came in together. But they did their own things after they got here."

"Did they argue?"

He shook his head. "Bob talked with friends; Hannah danced."

"Bob says she left with a couple. You see them go?"

"I was busy at the bar, but I saw them. I liked to watch Hannah. Always interesting. Bob didn't look happy about the couple, but when Hannah made up her mind to do something, she did it, and always with a smile, you know? She kissed Bob before she left."

"No fight?'

"No."

"How about the couple? Did they talk with Bob?"

He took another pull from his beer, emptied it. "The guy—he was around your age—he backed off like he didn't want to mix it up with Bob. Not that I blame him. But the girl—younger, good body—stayed next to Hannah, holding her hand. The girl kissed Bob, too. And then Hannah left with them."

"Did Bob stick around after they left?"

He shook his head and gave a little smile. "He followed them out."

"You told this to the police?"

"Yeah."

"You got any ideas about who killed her?"

"I've thought about it a lot," he said. "I never heard a bad word out of Hannah. She did what she wanted to do, you know? But she never hurt anyone. Never."

"Thanks for the help," I said, though I didn't see how he'd done me any good. "Hold on to my card, okay?"

He blinked mist from his eyes and slipped my card into his pocket.

SEVEN

MOM LIVED IN A yellow bungalow on Leland. It was
a one-story house, but Dad built a stairway and converted the attic into a bedroom, mine until I left home.
Mom kept the house scrubbed clean and the little front
lawn cut short. She'd trimmed two boxwoods outside
the front door into little balls. The only plant life that
wasn't trimmed tight was a tall, skinny white pine in
the front corner of the yard, and even it looked nervous.

As I got out of my car, my cell phone rang. Bill Gubman was checking in with the latest on Ahmed Hassan's
killing. I leaned against my car in the neat little driveway next to Mom's neat little yard and listened. "Hassan
choked to death on his own blood," Bill said. "I'm surprised you didn't hear the gurgle. The bullet that hit him
in the neck ruptured an artery and lodged in his throat.
The bleeding was mostly internal; otherwise, the place
would have been even more of a mess than it was."

He'd assigned a cop named Lucinda Juarez to watch the DVDs from the box the deliveryman dropped. I knew Lucinda and liked her. "I've seen a couple of the DVDs. Mostly amateurish stuff. Probably fifty or sixty hours of it," he said. "You want to come in and look at some mug shots on the chance you'd recognize the delivery boy?"

"Any shots of a guy in a brown jumpsuit and a yellow baseball cap? Because that's as good as you're going to get from me."

Instead of arranging a time for me to go down to the District Eighteen station, we confirmed dinner at his house on Friday.

MOM'S A SMALL, THIN woman, her hair all gray now. Like usual, she had on jeans and a blue cotton work shirt. She hugged me, her arms as strong as those of a woman four times her size. The house smelled like kielbasa, the kind of smell that makes strangers stop on the sidewalk and wish they were invited.

Two cheap plaid suitcases stood against the wall in Mom's kitchen. A tag on one said SOPHY MEZYK.

"I thought Sophy went back to Miami," I said.

"She did. Yesterday." Mom pulled a pot out of the oven. "You know, Sophy's getting old, Joe. She's having a hard time taking care of things." Sophy was born exactly a year after Mom, but she looked five years younger.

"She forgot her suitcases?"

"She doesn't have the energy she did when she was

raising Alexi." Alexi was Sophy's wild daughter. She'd just run off to live with a guy who worked at the Port of Jacksonville, dumping her eleven-year-old son on Sophy. That's why Sophy had brought Jason to visit: change the scenery, show him some people who loved him, fatten him up on Mom's pierogi.

A thump came from deep in the house.

Mom pulled out three dinner plates.

Another thump, like a baseball thrown against wall plaster.

I watched her spoon food onto each plate.

Thump.

I worked out what the thumping meant more slowly than I should have. Mom filled three glasses, two with water, one with milk.

Footsteps pounded down the stairs, and a tall eleven-year-old with a bowl haircut and big dark eyes ran into the kitchen clutching a tennis ball. "Hi, Joe."

"Hi, Jason." I gave him a hug, but I frowned at Mom.

We ate dinner and talked about the Cubs and the Florida Marlins. Since Sophy and Jason had arrived, almost all my conversations with the kid had been about baseball. Far as I could tell, he thought about nothing else. But after dinner, he dug into one of the suitcases and pulled out a football. He went out to the backyard to practice throwing it into a laundry basket.

When the back door had closed, I frowned at Mom again. "Your surprise?"

She gave me big eyes.

"You're too old to take in an eleven-year-old boy."

"I knew you would say that."

"You act like you're thirty years old, but you—"

"You're right."

"You can't do this on your own."

"I said you're right."

Then I knew she'd trapped me.

Mom took my plate and hers to the sink. "Sophy thinks it would be good for Jason to be around a man."

"And you told her that was a bad idea."

"I didn't."

"It's a bad idea."

"Don't disappoint him," she said. "He's had enough disappointment."

"He already thinks this is going to happen?"

"Sophy had to explain why he was staying."

"And when were you planning to tell me?"

"I'm telling you right now." She seemed angry with me, like I was being unreasonable. "It happened fast, Joe. We needed to decide what would be best for Jason."

"What kind of time are you talking about?"

"I'll take him weekends."

I shook my head. "You think he's going to stay with me?"

"He can't stay here," she said.

"No."

"He reminds me of you when you were a boy, Joe. Thin-skinned. A little soap in your ear, and you screamed like your hair was on fire."

"I still do that."

"You felt things more than most children. Not just pain. Things like loss." I must have grimaced, because she said, "You still feel it, but now you pretend nothing ever hurts. And you *are* stronger than you were. But if you're strong, that's something your dad gave to you. Me, too, but especially your dad. Jason needs someone like your dad right now."

I didn't want to say it, but I did. "Me."

"You."

I thought about the only kid I'd known recently: Kevin Morales, dead and broken on his mother's kitchen floor. "This isn't a good time."

Mom said nothing.

"I'm out working nights and days. Half the time, the fridge is empty. I bring women home and—"

She rolled her eyes.

"I do. Sometimes. Anyway, I don't have a lot to give to an eleven-year-old."

"Anything you give is more than he's got right now."

I shook my head.

"You owe it to him," she said.

"Alexi owes him. His father, wherever he is, he owes him. Sophy owes him. I don't owe him anything."

"Do it for me. And your dad."

She must've known mentioning Dad would do the trick, and so she'd saved him for last.

I shook my head, got up, went to the refrigerator, and opened a Coke, wishing it were bourbon. Mom stayed where she was, but she followed me with her eyes. "Stop doing that," I said.

A calm smile. "You're doing it to yourself."

"Now you're a hypnotist? Cut it out."

She said nothing.

I took the stare as long as I could stand it. "How long?"

She shrugged. "Two or three weeks."

"Fine."

"Could be a month or two."

"Two or three weeks. No more. Who will take care of him when I'm working?"

"He's in school during the day; after school, he's used to taking care of himself."

"Who will feed him?"

"I'll put some food in your fridge. You just put out a dish and a bowl of water in the morning; then you won't have to worry about him for the rest of the day."

"Cut it out," I said.

She came over and kissed my forehead. "Thank you, Joe."

"Sure," I said.

EIGHT

IN THE CAR ON the way to my house, Jason slouched against the passenger door and stared at the road.

"You okay?" I asked.

Nothing.

"Why so unhappy?"

Nothing.

"Look, I've got ways of making you talk." Still nothing. So I whistled the theme music to *The Andy Griffith Show*. It didn't seem to get on his nerves. "You upset about your mom?"

He shook his head.

I whistled the theme song some more.

"Stop," he said.

I kept at it.

"Please?"

"Why are you upset?"

"Why don't you want me to stay with you?"

So much for quarterback practice. He must've stood by the back door and eavesdropped.

I could have told him about Kevin Morales. I could have told him I was afraid, for him and for me. I said, "Think about happy things and you'll feel better, okay?"

He didn't look up. He said, "Thanks, Mary Poppins."

But when we drove into my garage, he was crying. I pulled him close to me and held him in my arms. After a while, I said, "Look, it's going to be okay. We're going to do this. All right?"

"All right." He didn't sound convinced. But I figured I didn't, either.

After my divorce, I bought a two-bedroom handyman's special in Ravenswood. I could turn a screwdriver as well as the next guy, and I knew if I didn't fill my time right, I would start turning the caps off bourbon bottles again. So I made the down payment, moved my clothes, a lamp, my stereo, and a TV from the house I'd shared with Corrine, and got to work. The first six months, I ripped out carpet and rotten floorboards, pulled down wet plaster, and replaced old pipes with PVC. At one point, you could stand on a chair and look through holes in the walls straight from the back bedroom through the dining room and out the living room window in the front. Now I was putting the place back together one room at a time. It didn't look as bad as a crack house anymore, but *Metropolitan Home* hadn't come to the door asking to do a photo spread yet.

I showed Jason around the house; then we sat at the kitchen table and I offered him a glass of milk. What else do you offer an eleven-year-old when he moves into your life? "In the morning, we'll go to your school," I said. "Coonley Elementary. Right in the neighborhood. Great place. Kids love it."

"How do you know?"

"Don't mess with my enthusiasm, okay?"

He gave me a blank stare.

It took me about three seconds to break. "The kids look happy when they're out at recess, all right? I don't know about inside. Could be torture in the classrooms and poison salami for lunch. But outside, everyone's happy."

He shrugged.

"After school, we can toss a football in the alley behind my house. Or play baseball, if you want."

He nodded a little.

"Yeah, we're going to make this work."

He stared at me like he was waiting to see what else I had to offer.

I didn't have anything else. "Okay, it's ten o'clock. Bedtime."

He looked at me, hesitant, but didn't argue. "Can I sleep in my Batman pajamas?"

"Of course," I said.

He got up, then hesitated at the door. "Thanks for letting me stay with you."

"Sure," I said.

"Because—Can I tell you something?"

I nodded.

"Because I love you more than my mom." He disappeared into the hallway.

I barked an uncomfortable laugh. I wanted to call

him back into the kitchen and tell him it wasn't true. He didn't even know me. I wanted to tell him he was a confused eleven-year-old in a confusing world. But I figured he already knew that, or if he didn't, my telling him wouldn't make him know it. So instead, I called after him, "And brush your teeth!"

Ten minutes later, he came back. He had on a Batman suit about two sizes too small and a gray mask with little gray bat ears.

"The suit's okay," I said, "but the mask goes."

"Why?" His lips drew a hard line across his face.

"Because—What's it made of?"

He pulled a fabric bat ear away from his head and the elastic snapped it back. "I don't know. Rubber?"

"Rubber would suffocate you. Take it off."

"My dad gave it to me."

"I don't care. It comes off."

"My mom lets me wear it."

I shook my head.

Again the hard lips.

"Look, you can wear it for breakfast, all right?"

"All right." He sulked off to bed.

"This will never work," I said after the door closed.

I hadn't moved from the kitchen table by 11:15, when the phone rang. It was Bill Gubman, as close to excited as he ever got. "We've got a possible ID on the deliveryman. You want to take a ride?"

Jason was in the guest bedroom, sleeping. I thought of Kevin Morales and the other broken kids I'd seen in the last thirty years. I wanted to protect Jason from that. I knew I should go to bed and sleep with my door open in case he needed me during the night. I should wake up early and make him a breakfast of eggs and bacon. "How long will it take?"

"Two hours max," Bill said. "We'll run out to an office park by the airport, pick up the guy if he's there, go home if he isn't."

"'By the airport' is outside city limits."

"Yeah, the place is in Franklin Park."

"Who cares about jurisdiction?"

"What's jurisdiction?"

"You want me to identify the guy?"

"If you can."

I knew I couldn't. But Hassan's bloody-eyed face was stuck in my mind, and seeing the deliveryman hand-cuffed in the back of Bill's car would give me some peace. I tried to put Kevin Morales out of my mind and told Bill, "Give me a call when you're out front." I left a note for Jason with my cell phone number in case there was an emergency.

Twenty minutes later, I was sitting next to Bill in an unmarked black Ford Crown Victoria. We cruised along side streets, going fifteen miles an hour over the limit, gliding like a bird from the dark into the orange light of streetlamps and back into the dark.

"You figure out who's behind BlackLite Productions?" I asked.

"That's a weird thing. They're totally underground. No tax records. No listing in the Yellow Pages. National telephone directory doesn't give a number for them. They don't even have a Web site, though people on S-M chat boards like the videos."

"What are the DVDs like?"

"Lucinda says it's mostly soft-core stuff. No kids, no farm animals, nothing all that bad."

"Probably just trying to skip on taxes."

"Probably. But a company's got to advertise their product. Looks like these guys sell store to store out of the back of a van."

"A white van."

"You got it. Lucinda goes into Angel's Adult Video on LaSalle this afternoon, watches until the owner sells a jerk-off DVD to a minor, then busts him, tells him he can give information about BlackLite or ride downtown. He makes a couple calls and gets the Franklin Park address. Doesn't know the name of the deliveryman, but he sounds like our guy."

"I would've liked to see Lucinda turning the store owner over."

Bill laughed. "Yeah, the girl's tough."

Bill liked music the way I liked bourbon, but his taste was old school. He put on a Rolling Stones CD, and "You Can't Always Get What You Want" crackled out of cheap speakers in the back.

"You ever hear of Modest Mouse?" I asked.

He kept his eyes on the road, accelerated through a yellow light. "Modest what?"

"Mouse. It's a band."

"No," he said. He leaned toward me and sang along with Mick Jagger.

After twenty minutes, we drove into the forest preserve that separates Chicago from Franklin Park, and the orange streetlights glowed behind us like a city in embers.

After a while, I said, "My mom dumped her nephew on me. I've got him sleeping in the guest bedroom."

"What the hell?" He grinned, as if he expected me to hand him a cigar. Bill and Eileen's daughter was born right after they finished high school, and he'd always said I was missing something.

"Scares the hell out of me," I said.

"A kid can do that."

"Not yours. What's she, a doctor now?"

"Doing her residency in Ohio. And I worry about her every day. But they bend more times than they break."

"Yeah, I've heard it, but I worry about the ones who break."

He grinned some more and socked me on the shoulder.

We drove out of the forest preserve and into the industrial side of Franklin Park. The factories never closed at night, but even with parking lots full of cars and windows full of light, they looked gray and tired.

Bill flipped off the music and the headlights when we turned onto a service road that led into a park full of portable offices. Eighty or ninety offices were spread over a few acres: gray aluminum sheds without windows, jacked off the ground three feet, with makeshift wooden stairs. We stopped and rolled down our windows. A sign on each of them advertised GE CAPITAL MODULAR SPACE. Another sign warned CAUTION! EXPOSED ELECTRICAL CONDUITS UNDER PORTABLES.

Lightbulbs strung between flimsy poles lighted the narrow lanes like Christmas. If a strong wind came through, you could have plowed the place and planted corn the next morning.

We drove slowly down a street, windows open, looking for portable number 29, headquarters of BlackLite Productions. We found it in the middle of the next row. A white van, with a deep scratch where it had sideswiped a car outside Stoyz, was parked outside.

Bill parked across the lane at the end of the row, blocking one of the two exits. He got out of the car and started toward number 29, and I started after him, looking to make sure no one was watching us.

Bill pulled out his pistol, and his stride melted into a run. Not bad for a fat guy. Then I saw what he saw. A man had come out of the door of number 29. Jeans, a brown leather jacket, and a yellow baseball cap.

The man walked toward the van, his back to us. He walked slowly, but his stride looked stiff, tense, like he was keeping himself from running, and even before he spun, you knew he would spin. He spun, aimed a gun at Bill, and fired. He crouched low to the ground, shot again, and rolled under the BlackLite portable.

He was in the dark, down in the metal framing, plumbing, and electrical wires. In the light, we were easy targets. Bill pointed at his car, and we ran toward it. He pulled two flashlights out of his trunk and exchanged his pistol for an assault rifle.

We moved back toward the BlackLite office, checking under the other buildings. The flashlights showed coils of electric wire hanging down from the floors, empty Styrofoam cups, crushed cardboard boxes.

No shooter.

Bill ran back toward his car again, and I split toward the open end of the lane to close a circle around the guy.

Fear of open electrical conduits and exposed wires would drive the shooter out of his hole pretty fast, so I started down the lane after the third row. My flashlight showed nothing under the first three offices and nothing on the roofs. Then I heard shoes on the pavement behind me.

The man stood square across the lane, arms extended toward me.

He fired. Concrete dust kicked up at my feet. He fired again. I shot back and he disappeared under another building.

I sprinted another two rows. I was crouching on the wooden stairway of number 71 when Bill came running full speed around the end of the row. The guy came out from under an office fifty feet from me, as if we'd synchronized watches. He saw Bill before Bill saw him, and he pointed his gun and fired.

The bullet hit Bill in the stomach.

Bill kept running, four steps, five, six, like he didn't know he'd been shot, then bent and rolled headfirst onto the pavement.

The man drew back under the office. I shot at him. He fired back a bunch of times and then was gone.

Bill stared up at me as I came along beside him. A crooked smile spread over his lips. "Shit," he said.

"Yeah, shit."

"Get him." The crooked smile turned into a grimace.

Blood was soaking through his shirt, pooling red and black on the pavement under him. I looked at the office the shooter had crawled under, then at Bill's pale, sweating face.

"Get him," he said again, angry, and a tremor went through his big body. Ahmed Hassan had shuddered like that as he died.

I reached for my cell phone, then knelt in Bill's blood, wiped the sweat off his forehead, and dialed 911.

NINE

AN AMBULANCE AND SIX Forest Park police cars found us ten minutes later. Suddenly, the night was bright with flashing lights and loud with sirens and police radios. The paramedics stabilized Bill and put him in the ambulance, then slammed the door before I could climb in beside him. Twenty minutes later, Chicago cops started showing up in their cruisers. Like Bill and me, they had no business being there, but the Forest Park cops didn't argue. One of their own was down, and they'd come to pay witness.

A Chicago canine unit arrived, and soon dogs were barking and crawling under the portables, smelling the shooter's sweat and fear, but it was no use. The white van was gone. A cop asked me the license number, but I hadn't bothered to look. If Bill had, he wasn't able to tell it.

District Eighteen cops showed up a little later, the guys who knew Bill personally. They were angry at the gunman, at the world, at me. The Chicago cops who'd seen me the night before at Stoyz looked at me as if *I* had shot Bill in the stomach. I guess they needed someone to take out their rage on, and I was available.

Only a thick-necked detective named John Henkels from the Twenty-third District tried to take me down, though. We'd butted heads before when I screwed up his investigation of a robbery/murder, and I'd drawn more blood from him than he'd gotten from me. But now he came after me, looking like I was already finished business.

I didn't mind him coming. If he wanted to fight me to ease the pain of Bill's shooting, I was glad to fight him for the same reason. He got closer to me than he needed. "Word is you were involved in another shooting with the same perp last night. So you're just hanging around watching this delivery boy two nights in a row and this time Gubman gets shot?"

"You should get your facts straight before you make a fool of yourself, John. I rode out here with Bill."

"Fuck you and the facts," he said. "I know the story. But if it happens like you say—the guy comes out the door, his back to you, then turns and shoots—how does he know you're behind him?"

I answered slowly, talking to the slow. "He saw us before coming out."

He put a hand on my shoulder, like I might try to run. "But there's no window."

"No window, John. Security cameras. Two of them." I nodded at the two small cameras mounted on the corners of the BlackLite office roof, facing in both directions down the lane. I couldn't really blame Henkels for missing the cameras. Bill and I had missed them, too. Still, when Henkels loosened his grip on my shoulder and looked embarrassed, I pointed at the camera facing us and said, "You know what that camera's recording now? You. Making an asshole of yourself."

He tightened a fist.

I grinned at the camera as if I was saying, "Cheese." That could have been enough to make him wonder about punching me on video. He wasn't an idiot, just a jerk.

He put his fist down. "You're involved in this," he said in a half whisper. "And I'm going to get you."

I felt like punching him, too, but I walked away. I wasn't an idiot, either.

Lucinda Juarez arrived in her own car, wearing jeans and a yellow button-down shirt smeared with paint. She'd been at home when she heard that Bill got shot.

We hugged. She was short and heavy-boned, with black hair and black eyes that usually had fire in them, though right then they were full of tears. "Bill?" she said.

"Yeah, Bill." My eyes were full of tears, too.

"Is he—"

"He's going to be all right." I didn't know if I believed it.

"And you're okay," she said with more relief than I probably deserved.

"I rode out here in Bill's car. Can you give me a ride to the hospital?"

She nodded. "Let's take a look inside first, okay?"

We walked together into BlackLite Productions. She went straight for a plastic carton by the door. I sat down in an office chair and looked the place over. There were two computers, a bunch of disc burners, two security monitors, a file cabinet, and an office desk to go with the chair I sat in. A little hunting probably would produce enough records to find every video store that sold BlackLite videos. At the far end of the room was a mattress, a couple crates stuffed with sex toys, and two digital video cameras on tripods.

Everything was neat and orderly. Nothing except the sex toys said this wasn't a legitimate business. I looked through the file cabinet, but nothing pointed at the BlackLite owners. The top drawer had a section labeled "Talent" and a bigger section labeled "Scripts." The first three folders in "Talent" contained information about Amber, Anastasia, and Cindi—no last names— photos and lists of sex acts each woman was willing to perform on-camera and how many people she was willing to perform them with. The bottom drawer contained manuals for the video cameras and equipment, the computers, and the security system.

Lucinda came over with the plastic carton under her arm. "Ready?" she asked.

We walked to her car. "What's in the carton?"

"More DVDs," she said, like the idea depressed her. "But the cases and discs are titled in pen, and they don't look like the finished product. If there's rough footage on them, they might show our guy in the yellow hat or someone in charge who can identify him."

"Don't you think you should let the Forest Park cops keep this stuff?"

"No," she said. "I want to get this son of a bitch."

"Bill said he had you screening the stuff from last night."

"If I watch much more of it, I'm going to need someone to tie me up and spank me."

I had the feeling the someone she was thinking about was me. The shooting must have shaken her up.

AT 3:00 A.M., THE STREET outside Rush Oak Park Hospital looked like a Chicago police station parking lot. A couple dozen cop cars were double-parked at the curb. Most of the cops were inside, waiting for information about Bill, but five stood together outside, leaning against a cruiser. A couple of them smoked, though they weren't supposed to on duty. On a night when another cop gets shot, the rules relax, or no one cares if they don't.

They gave us cold stares when Lucinda parked her Honda Civic next to them. But then one of them recognized her and gave her a hug. "Bill's in surgery," he said.

"At least he's alive," she said.

"Last we heard."

"He dies, this is a death-penalty case," an old cop said.

A young cop in uniform spit. "I get my hands on the perp, it's death penalty even if Gubman lives."

The old cop looked at him like he pitied him, but he didn't put him down.

Right after we walked inside, Bill's wife, Eileen, rushed into the ER, escorted by two cops. She was pale, living a nightmare. A nurse came out and took her into a room behind swinging doors. Eileen didn't seem to see me and Lucinda, but a few minutes later the nurse returned and asked us to go with her. We followed her through the doors into a bright white hallway that led to a hushed room with soft chairs for people who might have to hear the worst news of all. Eileen sat huddled in the corner of an overstuffed sofa, looking like she expected to hear that news. She didn't say anything when we walked in, but when I sat next to her and put my arm around her, her lips screwed up and she let out a sound that was half cry, half bitter laugh. "He's retiring," she said. "If"—her voice cracked—"if that son of a bitch lives, he's quitting tomorrow. He is *not* getting in that car again. He is *not* going back to the station."

Lucinda pulled an armchair close, sitting knee-to-knee with her.

Eileen stared into her eyes, but I don't think she saw her. I think she saw only herself and Bill. "He is *not* going back," she said again, "because if he does," she added, whispering, "it will kill me." She shook her head. "And he would never want to kill me."

We sat silent for hours in the room, a timeless room with no windows, no clocks, a room of death, or, if you were very lucky, life.

Then a doctor came in. He looked exhausted, but I felt like he had the power of God, and all he had to do was say a word—*live, die*—and it would come to be. "Your husband is out of surgery," he told Eileen. She tried a hopeful smile, but he shook his head. "The bullet did some organ damage, and we couldn't remove all the fragments. The big danger now is infection. If he gets past that, he'll recover fully."

"And if he doesn't?"

The doctor tried his own hopeful smile. "What do we have to lose by being optimistic? C'mon with me. He'll wake soon." He took her to be with Bill when he opened his eyes.

When Eileen left, Lucinda wiped her cheeks with a sleeve. I opened my arms to her, but she said, "I'm going to work."

"You've been up all night. Call and say you're not coming."

"No way. Not when the shooter's free."

"You know the shift supervisor's going to send you home."

She shrugged. "Let him fire me for working."

She offered me a ride, but I wanted to be near Bill, so I settled into the sofa and waited.

Eileen came back and her face had hope in it, though her eyes said she'd been crying. "He doesn't look so bad," she said. "He wants to see you, too."

He had breathing tubes through his nose, tubes in his arms, tubes snaking under his medical gown. He looked like he could breathe underwater with no tanks, like he could crap without a toilet. Seeing him like that made me cry, too.

"Looking good," I said.

He laughed, or tried to. "I feel like shit."

"I know."

He was quiet a few seconds. "The doctors give me thirty-seventy odds."

"What the hell do doctors know?"

"Next forty-eight hours will tell. If I make it two days, they say everything will heal."

"I'll sit right here for the next two days, then," I said.

"The hell you will." He growled the words louder than a dying guy had a right to. "You get this bastard."

I nodded.

Then, quiet again, he said, "You'll watch Eileen and Annie for me?"

"You know I will."

He closed his eyes for a moment. "Eileen wants to bring Annie home from Ohio. I told her no, but she's going to do it." He stopped. I'd never seen Bill cry before. "You watch over them, all right?"

I nodded some more. "I won't need to. You will. You'll drive Eileen crazy watching her. You'll see Annie become a great doctor."

"Yeah," he said, "that's right," but he didn't sound like he meant it.

I squeezed his shoulder. "You still feel solid."

"Some things do even when they start to crumble inside," he said, and he closed his eyes again.

I watched him for a while, then told him, "I'll send Eileen back in."

"Yeah, do."

He didn't open his eyes to watch me go.

The ER lobby was bright with sunlight. Morning had come while the surgeons pulled bullet fragments from Bill's gut. Most of the cops were still waiting. I went outside and called Corrine on my cell phone. "Hey," she said softly when she heard my voice, "I saw you and Bill on the news. Is he going to make it?"

"Don't know. Still too early."

"Damn."

"Yeah."

"How about you? You going to make it?"

"Don't know that, either. I was fifty feet from the shooter. If I'd been quicker—"

"Don't do that."

"It's true."

"Yeah, and they said on the news, if you hadn't been there, Bill would have bled to death."

"The news doesn't know what they're talking about."

"I want to help, Joe. What can I do?"

"Can you give me a ride home?"

Forty minutes later, she pulled up at the curb.

After I told her about Bill's injuries, we rode without talking. She knew me well enough to let me have the quiet. It felt good to be with her in the car, surrounded by her smells, her calm. Not every guy would have called her beautiful anymore. She'd gotten thick in the hips. Her long dark hair was streaked with gray. She'd been digging in a garden and had dirt on her jeans and hands. But I liked to look at her. And almost all the time, I liked to be with her.

Then, a couple miles from my house, she asked, "When are you going to quit all this?" That had also been her question in the months before we'd split up.

"Soon. Real soon."

She glanced at me like she didn't believe it.

"What do you think of living on a motorboat in Florida?" I asked.

Another glance. "The same thing I think about guilt-less chocolate and multiple orgasms. It's a wonderful idea, but it'll never happen to me."

"What if I said I was going to close my agency and sell my house?"

She rolled her eyes.

"I mean it. I'm tired. With the money from the house, I could buy a boat in Florida. You could come."

She laughed. "Send me a plane ticket when you move."

Even after what had happened with Bill, that made me smile. I settled into the car seat. "Is it true about the multiple orgasms? Never?"

She nodded. "Never."

"Hmm," I said. "Have you ever done it on a boat?"

I invited her to come inside, but she needed to get back to work. So I dragged myself up the front steps. It was 11:25 on a cold September morning, and I was alive. That was something. I let myself into the house. Sitting on the living room rug in Batman pajamas was an eleven-year-old boy. He looked angry enough to kill me.

TEN

I SAT ON THE rug, up close to Jason. What could I say to him? Would an eleven-year-old understand what had happened to Bill? Would he understand my need to stay at the hospital? Would he understand why I'd forgotten that I had a kid waiting for me at home? Hell, I didn't understand it. Why should he? All he knew was that he'd been in my house less than three hours before I abandoned him. That was easy to understand.

He said, "I want to go home."

"I know."

"I don't like it here."

"I know. I don't, either."

"This isn't going to work."

"Maybe not."

"You're supposed to be a fucking influence on me."

"Where did you learn language like that?"

"Like *influence*? My mom's not an idiot. She's just irresponsible." He looked hard at me. "Whole family is."

"Not like *influence*. And anyway, you mean 'good influence.' I mean like *fucking*."

"You go out all night and forget to take me to school; then you tell me I shouldn't say *fuck*?"

A smile came to my face from someplace far away. "You're a smart kid. You're right: You belong in school."

"Fuck school," he said.

I took a shower and shaved. When I walked back into the living room, he hadn't moved. "What do you want for lunch?"

He was still sulking. "I'm not hungry."

"Eat something. It'll make you feel better." Now I sounded like Mom.

He shook his head.

I took his hand and led him into the kitchen. We went to the refrigerator, looked inside. "You want a hot dog?"

"I can't stay here with you."

"Okay, a couple Vienna beef dogs, with chips and two beers."

With the littlest smile, he said, "I'm too little to drink beer."

"I'm not going to give you bourbon, if that's what you're after."

"You have Coke?"

I nodded. "A dog, chips, and a Coke."

He sat on a bar stool by the kitchen counter.

When the food was ready, I sat next to him. "Look," I said, "a friend of mine got shot last night. A policeman. He's hurt pretty bad, and I needed to be with him."

He looked down at his hot dog. "I know. I saw you on TV."

"I'm sorry I wasn't here."

"I know," he said. Then he ate his lunch.

Right then, I thought, This is a kid I could love.

At one o'clock, we walked into Coonley Elementary and asked to see the principal. By two o'clock, we'd taken a tour of the school and peeked into a sixth-grade classroom. The principal said Jason could start school the next morning as long as he could show he had the necessary vaccinations. For the rest of the afternoon, he was mine.

"What's next?" he asked. The question had some fear in it.

If I took him with me to Rush Oak Park Hospital, I would have to introduce him to Bill and explain that this was what it looked like to die, or almost. If I took him to the District Eighteen station to find out the latest on Bill's shooter, I probably would end up making him sit at Lucinda's desk while I watched porn videos, looking for a guy I wouldn't recognize unless he happened to have on a yellow baseball cap. I figured Jason probably would like to play catch, but I didn't have that in me. So I said, "We're going to a museum."

A tattooed kid with dreadlocks sat at the information desk in the School of the Art Institute of Chicago. He'd kicked his feet up on the desk and was listening to music through earphones. When we walked up to the desk, he pulled an earphone out of one ear and gave a pleasant smile that said he was ready to help us however he could.

Bob Piedras had told me that Le Thi Hanh had dated one of her teachers, a man named Charlie Morell. I asked for his office, and the tattooed kid looked at a notebook. "Charlie. He's in the Art History Department, teaches Contemporary Asian Arts. Room three oh nine. He's got office hours today until three-thirty." He put the earphone back in before I could thank him.

Morell's office door was open, and he sat inside at a computer. Instead of an office chair, he had a little recliner that looked like a miniature La-Z-Boy, and instead of overhead fluorescent lights, he had two incandescent floor lamps. The furniture made a statement: Come in. take off your shoes. Let's talk about Chinese pottery. I kept my shoes on, turned Jason loose on an exhibit of student art, and knocked.

Morell looked about six feet tall, 180 pounds. He'd shaved off all his hair except for a skinny braided ponytail that fell halfway down his back. It looked like a pull cord on a toy. Maybe when it retracted, you could pull it and his mouth would open and shut; then he would dance a jig. But a certain group of students would have found him very cool. Some of them, like Le Thi Hanh, would have wanted to sleep with him. He had large dark eyes and a big smile, which he flashed at me as I stepped into his office.

When I introduced myself as a PI, he said, "You're investigating Hannah's death?"

I admitted I was.

He crossed his hands in front of him and shook his head, as sad as an undertaker. "Poor Hannah." His hands were surprisingly small.

"Yes, poor Hannah. I hear you dated her."

The hands came apart, he gestured to a chair, and he closed his office door. Behind him were two black metal bookshelves lined with books on Asian arts. He had no art on the walls, which seemed strange for an art history professor, but maybe having no art was a statement about art, just like having a bald head was a statement about hair.

"I wouldn't say we were dating," he said.

"You wouldn't say it because you won't get tenure if you say it, or because you really weren't dating?" He looked nervous, so I said, "The door is closed, Professor Morell."

"Yes," he said, "let's keep it that way. I slept with her for a few months. But our relationship was about playing and playacting. And about conversation—"

"As opposed to dating."

"As opposed to—" He closed his eyes for a moment. "Did you know her?"

I said I didn't.

"Perhaps you had to. I met her when she took a course I teach on Art and Material Culture. She liked to play games. Every day, she came to class in a little skirt and a T-shirt with a different slogan on it. The first day it was 'Baby Doll.' I remember that. Then it was 'Party Favor.' Then 'Satisfaction Guaranteed.' She sat in the front row with a pen in her mouth and never took notes. She made it damn hard to teach. And she was smart. Did well on the tests. Wrote stunning essays. Then one afternoon, she came to see me in my office, and our relationship started."

"Old story: professor screws student."

"Why did you come to see me?"

"The police suspect my client in Hannah's murder,

and he hired me to investigate others who could have been involved."

"Is your client Bob Piedras?" I didn't answer, but my surprise must have shown. "It's not like you're the first person to talk to me about this," he said. "The police asked about my relationship with Hannah, and I told them it ended around the time she started seeing Bob. They seemed very interested in that."

"Do you know Bob?"

"I've met him once or twice." He shrugged. "No hard feelings."

"Did you tell the police you thought Bob killed Hannah?"

"Me? Hell no. I wouldn't tell them that even if I believed it, you know what I mean?"

"No," I said. "What do you mean?"

He settled back into his chair. "Let me put it this way: You go to a museum, and there's a painting of a female nude. What do you do? You stare at her ass and her breasts. You can use lots of fancy language to talk about the picture, but it's just an excuse for looking at a girl's ass and breasts. And what does she do when you look at her?"

"Nothing. She's a painting."

"Exactly. She's passive. You can look until you give yourself a heart attack."

"Cut the lecture, okay?"

"I'm trying to tell you something about Hannah."

"Then tell it."

"Hannah wanted to turn the tables. So she played games. She stared back, if you will."

"If I will what?"

Morell stared at me tight-lipped, like I was an especially slow student. Then he said, "That's what sitting in my class with the pen in her mouth was about. Legs spread just enough, you know? She was accusing me, looking at me and daring me to admit that I was looking at her. And she was right, of course. She played elaborate games like that, sometimes very cruel games. She made people watch her and she made them confront themselves for watching. She got off on that."

"She was an exhibitionist."

"I would use a different word. She made people look at her, yes, but she also made them look at themselves looking at her. For me, it was interesting. But some people don't like to see themselves that way. When people realized Hannah had set them up, they got angry with her. Sometimes very angry. Occasionally violent. She got off on that, too."

"So you're saying she had it coming? She deserved to get killed?"

"I'm saying she should have seen it coming, and she probably did."

"Then why didn't she stop? Why wouldn't she get out of the way?"

"It's possible she wanted it to come."

I didn't understand that at all. "And you were her lover."

He nodded. "Her lover, if you will"—he tried a quick grin—"though I would call myself her 'collaborator.'"

I thought about how she'd left Club 9 with the couple on the night she got killed, setting up the scene so Bob would see her go with them. "Did she set you up so you could see her with Bob Piedras? Is that how you know who he is?"

He laughed, uncomfortable. "So I could hear them anyway. She called me sometimes when Piedras was screwing her. To make me listen."

"How did you feel about that?"

"It didn't surprise me. It was typical Hannah. It's what she did."

I kept my eyes on him, let him grow uncomfortable with the silence.

He broke fast. "If you're thinking I killed her because I was jealous, you don't know me. I found Hannah interesting and enjoyed being with her, but I felt no jealousy."

I shrugged. "I don't know if I believe you."

ELEVEN

OUT IN THE HALL, Jason was talking with a couple of girls twice his age. They treated him like the cute little boy he was, but he was flirting with them. I said, "Ready, Jason?"

"Ready, Joe," he said, and he walked off with a swagger.

We drove up Lake Shore Drive toward Little Vietnam in rush-hour traffic. I called Rush Oak Park Hospital to check on Bill while we idled behind a pickup truck. Eileen picked up the phone in his room and said he was sleeping.

"Sleep is good," I said.

"Anything is good if he's still breathing."

Next, I called Lucinda at the District Eighteen station. "The BlackLite discs are rough cuts," she said. "I've heard directors setting up sex scenes, but no one has appeared on-screen except actresses and actors, and none of them has had on a yellow hat."

When we hung up, I called my office answering machine for messages. The judge had called to ask me to come back to see him at his house in the Dunes. Mom had called to tell me she was cooking a pot of *bigos* stew for Jason and me; she would stop by my house and leave it in the fridge. And the judge had left a second message, asking me to telephone him. I had nothing to tell him, so I erased that message along with the others.

Hannah's parents lived in a house on Kenmore in the block north of Argyle. The street was lined with concrete apartment buildings, three or four stories tall, buildings where the plumbing backed up into the bathtubs and the residents lined the windows and doors with rags to keep out the winter wind, though it was a waste of time and they were bone-cold anyway. Between the apartment buildings stood neat little brick and wood houses, freshly painted, windows washed, lawns cut, bushes trimmed. Hannah's parents owned one of those houses, just as neat as the others except that the lawn had gone a couple weeks without seeing a blade.

I parked a few buildings down, then went to the door with Jason and knocked. No one answered, though a light shined through blinds on a front window. I tried the knob, but the door was locked. A locked door wasn't a reason to stay outside, and I was curious what the drawers and closets would tell me about Hannah without protective parents keeping me from poking around in them.

"Are you going to break in?" Jason asked.

"That would be illegal."

He nodded. "Are you going to do it?"

I'd already exposed him to child abandonment; I didn't

need to try him out on burglary. Besides, in the yard next door, a tall old black man was watering a flower garden with a hose, and he looked neighborly enough to object to my popping the lock.

I knocked again, louder this time. Nothing.

The man next door turned off the hose and wandered over. "Can I help you?" he asked, none too friendly. He was seventy at least and his neck jutted forward like a waterbird's, but his arms were still muscled.

Jason eyed the man nervously. I stuck out my hand to shake. "I'm Joe Kozmarski and this is my cousin. We're looking for Mr. and Mrs. Le."

He ignored my hand. "They've seen enough trouble lately. They don't want to talk right now."

"They hire you to keep away groupies?"

He stepped in closer. "I'm their neighbor and a friend. And you"—he pointed at the bulge in my jacket where my Glock was—"you're carrying concealed. We don't like that around here."

If I ever moved into a rough neighborhood, I would want this guy on my block. I stepped in closer, too. "I'm a private detective investigating their daughter's death. If you're their friend, you'll tell me where I can find them. If not, then maybe you'll go back to watering your marigolds."

He didn't back off. "You got an ID?" I showed it to him, and I guess he liked what he saw. "Okay," he said. "You working for Bob Piedras?"

Hannah's ex-boyfriend at the Art Institute knew Bob, and so did her parents' neighbor. "How do you—"

The tall man smiled. "Mr. Piedras introduced himself

after Hanh got killed. He asked me to keep an eye on her parents, make sure they were okay. I told him I was already doing that. He seems like a good man."

"Yeah," I said, "Bob's a saint. The parents doing okay?"

"Far as I know, considering. Week after the funeral, they left town to stay with relatives in New Jersey. Don't know when they'll be back or if."

"They run a store nearby, don't they?"

"Nam Hai. It's still open. Around the corner on Argyle. The sons run it. Lanh and Chinh."

"They live in the house with their parents?"

"Nah, they've got the apartment over the store. They're young guys, you know? And young guys've got to have space." I thanked him for the help, and he shook his waterbird head. "Hanh was a sweet girl." He pointed at Jason. "I knew her since she was about this guy's age. Her dying like this broke her parents' heart."

He wandered back to his garden.

A clerk in the grocery store said the Le brothers weren't there, so Jason and I climbed the stairs next to the store. The paint on the stairway walls was yellow and peeling, scribbled with black-marker graffiti. The steps were bare wood and sagged under my weight. Jason trotted up behind me like he'd been here before. At the second-floor gangway, in front of the single apartment door, a cockroach was lying with legs in the air. Jason leaned to inspect it while I knocked.

When the door opened, a skinny, stringy-haired kid in his twenties greeted us. He had bare feet, black pants, and a ribbed sleeveless gray T-shirt that showed off arms and shoulders that seemed to have no muscles at all. In his hand was a ten-inch hunting knife.

Jason smiled up at me like he was glad I'd brought him along for the ride. I put my hand on his shoulder and said to the man in the door, "Were you expecting a deer?"

He held the knife loosely, but with a flick of the wrist, he could have it at my neck. Or Jason's. "What do you want?"

"I'm a private detective," I said, "and I'm investigating your sister's death, if you're Lanh or Chinh."

"Chinh," he said. "And the cops already came."

"Have they arrested anyone for killing her?"

"No."

I felt the bitterness. I showed him both palms. "That's why I'm here."

He opened the door wider and motioned us in with the knife blade.

The foyer led into a big room with two bedroom doors on the back wall. The floor was brown vinyl tile and needed washing. A couple of windows let in the noise of traffic from the street below. An old green couch faced a large-screen TV, and behind the couch hung a poster for a movie called *Cyclo*, which looked like it had plenty of guns and at least one very pretty Vietnamese actress. A fridge, a sink, a microwave, and a dining room table pushed against a wall counted as the kitchen.

Another man sat at the table eating a McDonald's Quarter Pounder and sipping a large Coke. He could have been Chinh's twin except he weighed about forty pounds more—all muscle—was about four inches taller, and had a crew cut. And he didn't have a hunting knife. He didn't look like he needed one.

"Lanh?" I asked.

He nodded.

Chinh said something in Vietnamese, and his brother pointed at a couple of empty chairs.

"Sit down," Chinh said. He set the knife on the table.

Lanh tipped the carton of fries toward us. Jason took a couple.

"My client suggested that I talk to your parents about Hannah, but when I went by their house—"

I stopped short. Chinh looked at me as if I'd called his sister a whore. "Her name isn't Hannah," he said. "It's Hanh." He looked to see if I had a problem with that.

"Right," I said, "my client suggested that I talk to your parents about Hanh—"

"Who's your client?" Chinh asked.

"Bob Piedras."

Chinh reached for the knife on the table.

I turned to Lanh. "Having a sister killed could turn anyone into a jumpy poodle, but would you put a leash on him before he hurts himself?"

Lanh took a bite of his Quarter Pounder, said nothing.

Chinh said, "We know what happened to Hanh, okay?"

"Tell *me* what happened," I said. "I don't know."

He looked at me as if I was lying. "We'll take care of this ourselves."

"Next, you're going to start humping my leg, aren't you?"

Chinh was skinny and had no muscles, but in a flash he held the knife to my throat. The blade didn't touch me, but my skin flushed.

"Please put down the knife, Chinh."

Lanh watched, distant.

Chinh fanned the knife back and forth across my neck. Its wind sent a chill through me. The weight of my gun rested inside my jacket. If the blade touched me or if Chinh turned it on Jason, I would shoot him.

"Put the knife down," I said as calmly as I could. I think my voice cracked.

He brushed it closer.

Jason stood up suddenly and shouted, "Put it down, asshole!"

Chinh turned, surprised, uncertain.

Lanh laughed from the belly, then put his hand on Chinh's wrist and lowered the knife to the table. "It's okay, little man," he said; then to me: "Look, my sister's been dead just three weeks. She'd moved away from our family a couple years ago, and my parents had stopped talking to her. Me and Chinh, we barely talked to her, either. And now it's too late. So you understand, we've got to take care of this ourselves."

"I want to help," I said.

Lanh shook his head. "Thanks, but we'll do it."

"With a knife?"

"Whatever it takes."

"Is the rest of your family in on this, too, or is it just you guys?"

"My parents are old," he said. "They're mourning for Hanh. And for themselves. That's enough for them right now."

Bob had mentioned an older brother, an estate lawyer living on Chicago's Gold Coast. "And your other brother?"

"Tuan? He's not part of the family right now."

"If you don't stay near home and help run the store, you don't get to be part of the family?"

He nodded, as if this was logical. "That's pretty much it, yeah."

"Your sister was mixed up in a pretty wild life. A lot of sex and drugs. Are you sure you want to bring all that home with you?"

"We know who our sister was. We'll be able to handle it."

I gave him my business card and told him to call if he needed help or if he could help me. Jason and I started toward the door.

Lanh dug a couple fries out of the bottom of the carton with big fingers. "Watch out for your little partner," he said. "He's got balls." He pointed his thumb at Chinh. "Big balls get little guys in trouble."

"Asshole," Jason muttered as we left the apartment.

A couple buildings from the Le's store was Café Nhu Hoa, the best Laotian restaurant in the city. Mom's *bigos* would hold for a day, so I took Jason out for duck *laap, tam mak houng* salad, and barbequed *som moo*.

When we sat down, Jason said, "That was cool." He had wide, excited eyes, an eleven-year-old on adrenaline.

"Never confront someone with a weapon," I said. "Never, unless you're ready to back yourself with muscle of your own."

"All he had was a knife."

"Knives cut, especially big knives. You don't play with them. Didn't your mom teach you that?"

"But you have a gun. You could've shot him."

"I could have, yes, but I didn't want to. I don't like to shoot people, okay?"

"Okay." He looked at me like he couldn't see why not.

The *tam mak houng* came, and I warned him about the spice. But he showed no fear of it, either.

"Also," I said, "I don't want to hear any more of the language."

"You mean 'asshole'?"

"That's what I mean."

"I got him to put down the knife."

"Yeah, I know, but I don't want to hear it."

"Okay," he said, and he ate a slice of papaya dotted with hot chilies.

After dinner, we wandered back toward my car. Twenty yards behind us, a battered red sedan rolled slowly along the street, keeping near the curb. The windows were down, and the occupants didn't hide that they were following us. Chinh Le drove, and Lanh sat in the passenger seat.

The car stopped when we got into my Skylark, then started in behind us again when we pulled from the curb. It followed us through the city streets as we drove toward Ravenswood. It passed only when we pulled into the alley beside my house.

TWELVE

I SLEPT HARD TILL early morning, then dreamed of Kevin Morales. Again, he was lying broken on the kitchen floor, one leg twisted back at the knee. His mother drank coffee and ate scrambled eggs next to her dead child's body. I let myself in when no one answered my knock. I saw the boy and said, "What's wrong with Kevin?" A stupid, stupid question every time I asked it. I knew what was wrong with Kevin. Kevin was dead. And, every time, I tried to lift Kevin, but I couldn't. He was heavier than the house where his mother had killed him. But this time, I did it: I lifted him, and he weighed the same as a child, no more, no less. I lifted him and held his cold body in my arms. It seemed as if I were flying, it felt so good to hold him.

I woke up. It was 5:30 in the morning, and Jason was still sleeping in the next room. It was too early to call Bill's room at the hospital. So I put on shorts, running shoes, and a sweatshirt and let myself out of the house.

The northeast wind had blown itself out, and the morning was cool and clear. I ran two miles toward the lake, south through the lakefront park, and then back toward my house. As I completed the run, I passed a red Dodge Dynasty almost as old as my Skylark, though it looked like it had gotten less love. Chinh and Lanh were sleeping inside, Chinh spread across the front seat, Lanh across the back. Asleep, they didn't look as peaceful as Jason, but they also didn't look like they would knife you for the fun of it.

I rapped on the car roof with my fist and watched them jump back to life. Then I jogged back to my house. Some guys can't be competent thugs unless you help them.

I got Jason out of bed, and while he was showering, I called Bill's room. Eileen answered. After midnight, Bill had developed a fever, and infection had set in. The doctors had wheeled him back into surgery at 5:00 A.M. He hadn't regained consciousness. All we could do was wait and see. While I'd been dreaming happy dreams, he was dancing toward death.

I said I would drive over to the hospital, but Eileen said no. Their daughter, Annie, was flying in from Ohio later in the morning, and until then, Eileen wanted to be alone. I managed to drop Jason off at Coonley Elementary without warning him that, foot on the brake, we were all speeding toward death. I gave him a key to my house and told him I would be home in time to make dinner.

Then I pointed my car downtown. The red sedan tailed me again, but I wasn't in the mood. As soon as we hit traffic, I changed lanes and put some cars between us, then left the sedan behind at a stoplight. Pounding on the car roof had wakened the Le brothers, but it hadn't taught them much.

I dialed Lucinda Juarez on my cell phone. She answered her phone, annoyed: "What?"

"Have a bad night?"

"Yeah, sorry. I've been up working."

"You still watching the DVDs?"

"All night long. This stuff has got me sweating, Joe."

"What are you going to do now?"

"I'm going home to try to sleep. Got any sleeping pills you want to share?"

"Not unless you want to sleep the whole day away. I used to do bourbon. A bottle will knock you out for a few hours, but I don't recommend it."

"Just don't recommend I rent a video."

"Maybe take a cold bath."

"I think I'll try a couple drinks and a hot bath."

"Don't drown."

"You'll like this," she said. "Forensics matched the slug we removed from the door frame in the Stoyz shooting with the bullets from last night."

"Which means the deliveryman killed Ahmed Hassan."

"Sure looks like it, though they're still working on the slugs taken out of Hassan."

"Okay, and why would the deliveryman shoot Hassan?"

"Hell if I know," she said.

"Right. Me, too. You working again tonight?"

"Watching more videos."

"If you want, you can bring some of them to my house, and I'll look at them with you."

"They're logged evidence," she said. "I can't take them out of the station."

"And Bill's in the hospital, dying."

"What time should I come by?" she asked.

We hung up when I turned onto Wabash, a block from my office.

The red sedan was waiting for me outside my building, parked in a loading zone. Must've taken a shortcut. Lanh was in the passenger seat, watching the morning crowd. Chinh was in the driver's seat, blowing smoke rings out the open window. That's what I got for giving Lanh my card.

I parked and walked back to their car, leaned against Chinh's door. Maybe we just needed to talk more, become better friends. "Would you boys like to come up to my office?"

They studied their windshield as if it were a Rembrandt and said nothing to me.

"I want you to stop tailing me," I said. "You're making me nervous."

A smile twitched at the edge of Chinh's lips.

"Not nervous like you worry me. Nervous like a bad itch. Can you at least tell me why you're following me?"

Chinh held his cigarette out the window and tapped the ash onto my shoe.

"Okay," I said. "I'll be in my office for about half an hour. That's enough time to get breakfast, if you're hungry. Grandma's Kitchen on the corner scrambles a good egg, but don't order the tuna fish."

The corridor to my office was full of students from the secretarial school. They looked ambitious and hopeful. They deserved better than a school that ate their government money and spat them back onto the street without jobs. I sometimes thought I would hire one of them if my business grew, but it never did, and anyway, they probably deserved better than me, too.

Inside my office, my answering machine blinked red. I punched the play button and the judge talked to me: "Come back to the Dunes this morning at ten, okay? You can meet Bob's lawyer. Sanke's getting involved in the case now, and I'd like you to work with his security and investigation staff."

I ignored the call and turned on my computer. I brought up Google and typed in "Le Thi Hanh." A tour company in Hanoi had an operations director named Le Thi Hanh. Another Le Thi Hanh was treasurer of a group called the Australia Club. And a sociologist named Le Thi Hanh studied women's poverty in Third World countries. But except for a one-paragraph *Chicago Tribune* article about her murder, the Internet didn't know a Le Thi Hanh who studied art, partied too hard, and tormented ex-lovers in Chicago. Same thing if I substituted the name Hannah for Hanh. Nothing at all if I added the names Chinh or Lanh.

Entering "Charlie Morell" and "Charles Morell" gave me a nineteenth-century author and also an assistant professor at the School of the Art Institute of Chicago who had written an article on Chinese ceremonial robes and another article on Thai textiles.

Typing "Bob Piedras" and "Robert Piedras" gave me

four hits, all for my friend and client. No one online was nominating him for sainthood, but almost. Turned out the boy was a regular churchgoer. Three sites showed he served on the Liturgy Council at Holy Name Cathedral. So he partied all night at Club 9 and then went to Mass in the morning still smelling of the sins he had to confess. The fourth site made me sink back in my chair. It said he had participated in a silent auction held by the cathedral. The article came up with a picture of him and his purchase. I studied the picture. He had bought a Chinese ceremonial robe for eight thousand dollars. It was big and bright blue, with gold stripes on the sleeves and silver dragons on the front. What would he do with a robe like that, and why would he want it eight thousand dollars' worth? How did the purchase connect to Charlie Morell's article on Chinese robes? I needed to ask Bob how well he knew Morell.

If Donald Sanke and his people were at the judge's, Bob probably would be there. I locked my office door, went downstairs, and saluted Chinh and Lanh, then drove south out of the city, dragging the red sedan behind me.

THIRTEEN

BOB WASN'T AT THE judge's house, but Sanke, a couple legal assistants, and Sanke's security team were hanging out in the living room. The judge's Realtor friend, Carla, lay on a recliner on the patio outside the living room window, soaking up the sun.

Sanke sat in the middle of the judge's old leather sofa. He had bleached teeth, a tanning-booth tan, and thinning brown hair that he'd gelled over his scalp. He had a gold watch on one wrist, a thick gold bracelet on the other, and a thin gold chain around his neck. If you took X-rays, you probably would find gold inside him, too.

He hopped up and shook my hand as if he'd been waiting his whole life to meet me.

"Where's Bob?" I asked the judge.

Sanke flashed a bleached white smile and answered for him. "My friends in the state attorney's office say they'll indict Mr. Piedras this afternoon or tomorrow morning, a little earlier than we were led to expect. I've advised him to lie low. We'll bring him in when we're ready, not when the state attorney says he wants to see him. Everything from now on is a game of tug-of-war. They make us work for every inch, and we make them work for every inch."

"Donald is calling the shots now," the judge said. "If he tells Bob to stick his head in the sand, Bob will eat and breathe beach until Donald tells him to come up for air." I knew where the judge was headed. "Everyone needs to coordinate efforts through Donald, and that means you'll answer to Ben Turner, the head of his security and investigation staff." He gestured to Turner, who was sitting in an armchair with a tumbler of vodka. He was a big man with short graying hair. He didn't smile or frown or do much of anything with his lips, not even when he was drinking.

"Two days ago, you hired me to work on my own," I said.

"Two days ago, it looked like we had more time," the judge said. "The state attorney is treating this more aggressively than we expected. Donald thinks a unified effort will work best."

"Sorry," I said, "I don't work well with others."

The judge smiled at that. He knew from personal experience that I had a problem taking orders. My problem had caused him big trouble a long time ago. "This is for Bob, okay?" he said. "Just talk to Ben and then decide."

Turner patted the cushion on the chair next to him and talked to me like I was a terrier. "Sit down, and we'll bring you into our plan."

I didn't sit down, but I also didn't piss on his leg. "What's the plan?"

"Simple. We find the man who killed Le Thi Hanh, and"—he threw a meaty fist into an open hand—"we bring him in." His lips hardly moved when he talked.

"Simple," I said.

He nodded.

"You mind opening your mouth a little?"

"Why?"

"I want to see if you've filed your teeth into points."

Turner lifted his eyebrows at the judge.

The judge put a hand on my shoulder. "Please work with the man. He's one of the best."

"I'm sorry, Judge."

He said to the others, "Give us a couple minutes," and guided me out a glass door onto the patio. The pool dazzled in the sunlight. There were potted flowers and a small pool house on one side and more potted flowers on the other. There were assorted wooden deck chairs and a gas grill big enough to cook hot dogs for a ballpark. Carla Pakorian smiled and waved her little finger at me from one of the chairs. I waved a little finger back as the judge led me toward the pool house.

He gazed at Carla lying in the sun. He gazed at the pool. He said, "The day I got suspended from the bench, you know where I went?"

"Where?"

"The Lincoln Park Zoo. The zoo—*me*—can you see it? Standing next to the old men feeding peanuts to the monkeys when the zookeepers weren't watching. Tripping over strollers. Then I started going every day."

"Why?"

"The polar bear."

"The polar bear."

"Yeah. You ever see him? He's absolutely crazy. They've got him in this little tank of water, about thirty by thirty, fifteen or twenty feet deep, fake rocks on the side, painted white to look like snow. Ball floating in the tank for him to play with. But he doesn't play with it; he swims back and forth, glass wall to glass wall, all day long. He hits the glass with his big paws, paws that could take your head off as easy as a guy flicks the ash off a cigarette. When he hits the glass, everyone jumps, and he swims to the other side. Back and forth. He's crazy. You can see it in his eyes. He can't take it, what they've done to him."

"Okay," I said, "but I still don't get it."

The judge looked me in the eyes. "I didn't want to be like him. I went to the zoo to remind myself of what I could become if I let them put me in a cage."

"I'm not refusing to work with Sanke because of our past. I'm refusing because I don't work with others."

"What I'm saying is I'm sorry. Those were bad days, running-scared days. I did a lot of bad things to the people I loved. Naming your dad to the investigators was one of the worst of them."

The judge's first betrayal.

"Did Dad really pass bribes to you?"

"Your dad? No. Never. I never even asked him, never would've. Your dad was the cleanest cop I ever knew."

"Then why did you name him?"

He shook his head as if confused. "The hell if I know.

They were pushing me for names, and I gave them names. I named . . . him. Hell if I know why. Maybe because he was so damned clean, and I wasn't."

I felt like punching him in the teeth. I thought about his second betrayal. I was a rookie cop at the time, and he asked me to pass him a bribe from the parents of a seventeen-year-old who'd been arrested for vandalizing a school building. A kid's prank, no worse than a dozen I'd pulled myself. So, I thought, Why not? He was Dad's oldest friend. He'd taught me how to fish. "Trust me," he said, "I won't name you if I get caught, and anyway, everyone's playing the game, and no one's getting caught." So I played.

And, in a funny way, he'd told the truth. I could trust him. He named Dad to the investigators even though he was clean, but he didn't name me. I didn't get caught. I still owed him something for keeping me out of the investigation. I always would.

But then fifteen years ago, he'd done something worse than breaking the trust. When Dad confronted him about naming him, the judge told him I was in it. Dad could handle losing his career, and he could even handle his best friend falsely accusing him. But learning that I was dirty broke his heart. I wouldn't forgive the judge for that.

"Why did you tell my dad I passed bribes?"

He looked at me straight. "I was still pissed off at you."

I knew why. After passing two bribes, I'd refused to pass a third. Even back then, I'd had a problem following orders. A burglar named John DeVries was convicted of robbing an apartment. My job was easy: take money from DeVries and give it to the judge before sentencing. But then I learned that DeVries had hurt a woman and her daughter in the break-in, but the prosecutor dropped the assault charges because the victims were too scared to testify. So I took DeVries's money but didn't give it to the judge. The judge didn't know what was up and he sentenced DeVries to the maximum. When the corruption investigations started, DeVries was the first to turn state's evidence.

"So why didn't you name me to the investigators?" I asked.

"I told you I wouldn't." He shrugged, as if it was simple. "You know, I've always loved you like you were my own kid."

I still wanted to punch him in the teeth, but the old man also made me want to cry. "Parents don't do what you did to me."

He shook his head. "Damned thing is, they shouldn't, but they do it all the time."

I looked at him. Trust me, his face said. Trust your old friend the judge.

"Why are you trying to slow me down by hooking me up with Sanke?" I asked.

"I'm not. I'm following the advice of one of the best criminal attorneys in the country."

"Why did Bob buy a Chinese ceremonial robe?"

"Huh?"

"A Chinese ceremonial robe. Like a samurai robe, but fancier. He bought one at a silent auction."

"Hell, I don't know. Ask him. For all I know, he wears leotards when he's alone. Who the hell cares?"

"Hannah's old boyfriend is an expert on the robes."

"I'm not following this, Joe."

"Bob hasn't told the whole story. He's connected through that robe to Hannah's old boyfriend. And I'm pretty sure he set up the bartender at Club Nine to give me a good line on him. He also went to visit Hannah's parents after she died; he's got a neighbor watching them for him. Hannah's brothers got spooked when I told them he was my client. Et cetera."

"What are you saying?"

"I'm asking what happens if it turns out Bob killed the girl."

"He didn't." The judge smiled. "I've known Bob as long as I've known you. I know what he's capable of, and I know he couldn't kill that girl any more than you could."

"I'm not convinced."

"Will you try working with Sanke's people?"

"I'll think about it."

"Okay. Just don't think too long. This is starting to move fast."

He walked back inside.

I watched the sunlight sparkle on the pool water, and I thought of about ten reasons why I should quit the job. Then I walked over and sat in a chair next to Carla. She had on jeans and a blue sleeveless blouse. She'd taken off her shoes and put them neatly together at the bottom of her lounger. Her tan was as natural as Donald Sanke's was fake. Her skin looked warm, and I wondered how it would feel to the touch. But below her elbows, her arms were blue with fresh bruises.

I nodded at the living room window, where the judge was talking with one of Sanke's legal assistants. "You trust the judge?"

She smiled a little. "Depends on the circumstances. In general, no."

"Why do you hang out with him?"

"I don't know. I guess he's good company."

"That's what he says about you."

She shrugged. "Yeah, it's an easy line."

"Are you sleeping with him?"

A little anger sparked in her face. "It's none of your business, but I could do worse than him."

"My guess is you spend time with him because you're scared."

She laughed, but less than she should have. "He's seventy-two years old. Even if he wanted to, he couldn't scare me."

"What happened to your arms?"

Again the little laugh. "I bumped myself on the fishing boat."

I shook my head. "The perch were biting, but not like that."

The judge waved at us out the window.

We waved back, all smiles.

"Did Bob kill Le Thi Hanh?" I asked.

"This isn't a good place to talk about these things."

"Seems private enough to me."

"If you drive toward the beach from here, you'll see five A-frame condos. Mine's the green one in the middle."

"When will you be there?"

"Anytime I'm not here." She closed her eyes and lifted her face to the sun.

"You're a very beautiful woman," I said. "If you're sleeping with the judge, he's a lucky man."

She said nothing to that.

I went back inside and sat next to Ben Turner like a good terrier. "At your service."

"Good." He nodded, but he didn't pat my head. "First of all, I want you reporting directly to me."

When we were done agreeing that I would do whatever I was asked to do, Turner and I walked outside to a Hyundai SUV. In the back were two cartons packed with spiral-bound telephone logs. They recorded all calls made from the Art Institute's Art History Department during the past year. Turner gave me the cartons and a sheet listing four phone numbers. He said, "I want you to check the logs for calls made to any of the numbers. There's a lot of material there, but it shouldn't take more than a day or two. All right?"

"Sure," I said, "happy to do it." I put the cartons in my trunk. Searching through the logs was grunt work. "This should keep me out of the way for a while, huh?" Turner looked at me as if he didn't know whether I was joking, so I added, "If I worked for a six-hundred-dollar-an-hour lawyer like Donald Sanke and I found out someone like me had been hired to help, I might give him a couple boxes of telephone logs, too." I slammed the trunk shut. When the roads got icy in a couple of months, the extra weight would help keep my bald tires from fishtailing. In the meantime, the cartons would sit in the trunk while I got back to work.

"You could do me a favor, too," I said.

"What's that?" he asked, as if he was afraid I was selling tickets to the fireman's ball.

"There're two guys sitting in a red Dodge Dynasty at the bottom of the judge's driveway. They're harmless, but they've been following me. Have one of your guys slow them down when I leave."

That was easier than getting hit up for twenty bucks. "No problem," he said.

"Also, I've got some questions I want to ask Bob."

He looked at me square. "Write them down and I'll get them to him."

"You want to give me his phone number?"

"You can write, can't you?"

"Only in crayon."

"Give them to me in crayon, then," he said, and he turned back to the house.

FOURTEEN

IF I COULDN'T ASK Bob about the ceremonial robe and his connection to Charlie Morell, I could ask Morell. At the Art Institute, the schedule of his classes and office hours posted outside his office door said he would return the next day at 3:00 P.M. So I visited the tattooed kid with dreadlocks at the information desk again. Like the day before, he had his feet kicked up on the desk and earphones in his ears. I grinned at him, and he pulled out both earphones and said, "You find Charlie yesterday?"

"Yeah, and I told him I would bring by some work I've done." I tried to look embarrassed. "But I couldn't get back last night until after he was gone, and now he's not in his office." I raised my hands; I was helpless and needed advice from an information expert.

"Why don't you go by his house?"

"Will a professor allow that?"

"Some do." He paged through his notebook. "Yeah, Charlie does." He gave me a Rogers Park address.

I thanked him and turned to go.

"Where's your kid today?"

"He's not my—" It wasn't worth explaining. "At school."

He waved an index finger in the air. "*Exactly* where children belong." He popped the earphones back in.

The address in Rogers Park was the bottom half of a yellow-brick two-flat building on a mixed street. Techno dance music pounded through the closed door and windows. I knocked and got no answer, knocked harder, then knocked again. I could fire my Glock into the thick wood door, which might get the attention of someone inside. Or I could work the lock and let myself in quietly.

I worked the lock.

The music led me down a hall past a big living room, a dining room, and a bedroom. The furniture was metal and blond wood and rode low to the floor. The hall ended at a small kitchen full of stainless-steel appliances. There were two doors in the kitchen. One went out to a small backyard. The music came from behind the other.

That door led down to a basement, dark except for a strobe light. The last time I'd seen a strobe light in a basement was at a friend's birthday party when I was twelve years old. I walked downstairs, hoping to find cake.

The basement was white: white carpet on the floor, white paint on the ceiling and concrete walls, three white couches. A girl straddled a guy on one of the white couches, her long blond hair draped over her shoulders and face like a cape, her black leather skirt hiked up almost to her hips, her bare feet taut with something that looked like pleasure. She kissed the guy hungrily. Under her, he was just a tousle of dark hair, jeans, and an unbuttoned blue shirt. His bare feet were as taut as hers.

Charlie Morell danced wildly by himself in the middle of the carpet. The sound was pummeling his body. The music was a techno chant, a mantra to the pleasure the couple was feeling on the couch. It was some of the best dance music I'd ever heard. Morell was lost in it. So was the couple. The guy had his hand up the girl's skirt. Soon he had her panties off. A groping Houdini, he managed it without her ever unstraddling him.

I walked past Morell to the stereo cabinet and turned off the tuner. Behind the cabinet were two light switches. I used them both. One turned on a big ceiling lamp and the other turned off the strobe. Morell froze in his dance, then fell to the carpet and didn't move.

I went to him and nudged him with my shoe to see if he was dead. The girl stopped kissing the guy and watched me. Then she climbed off him, came over, and did the same to Morell with a bare foot.

"What's wrong with him?" I said.

She looked at me like I'd crawled up out of the carpet. "He's extremely high."

"Is he all right?"

She looked him over. "I don't think so." Then she went to the stereo, started the music, hit the light switches, and returned to the guy on the couch, straddled him, kissed him.

Morell didn't move.

I went back to the stereo cabinet and pulled the speaker wires out of the tuner. I flipped on the lights so we could see. The girl shook her head, climbed off her partner again, and walked up so close, her toes almost touched my shoes. She smelled like sex. She also looked extremely high. "You're wrecking a good time," she said. "Do you mind?"

"What's Charlie on?"

"He did a few hits of E."

"A few?"

She moved in closer, like she'd decided she would straddle me when she got done with the guy on the couch. "Why do you want to turn off the music?"

"I don't want to turn off the music. I want the music to play all the time. I want you to do your lap dance, if that's what makes you happy. I want you to kiss your boyfriend like a cannibal. I want Charlie to dance by himself, if that's how he gets his kicks. Hell, I want to listen to music and dance, too. But I turned it off because a girl died, and I'm trying to find her killer."

She frowned and closed her eyes for a few seconds. "Shit," she said. "You wrecked the mood." She went to the couch and grabbed her panties, pulled them on under her skirt. Then she sat next to the guy on the couch, still frowning, her hand on his knee.

"You were friends with Hannah?" I asked.

She nodded, unhappy about it. "We hung out."

"You got a name?"

"Jamie."

The guy next to her wasn't happy, either, but he saluted me with two fingers. "Henry."

"I'm Joe Kozmarski," I said, and I flashed my license. "I'm working for Bob Piedras."

Jamie gave me more frown, which I took to mean she knew Bob and was voting against his sainthood. "Count on Bob to buy his way out of trouble."

"How's that?"

"He buys everything else: nice cars, drinks for everyone, drugs—"

"Sex?"

She nodded.

"You?"

She looked annoyed but said nothing.

"Hannah?"

One side of her mouth lifted in a sarcastic smile. "Have you seen her apartment?"

I said I hadn't.

"The Donatello Suites downtown. Investment bankers from London live there. Poor art students from Little Vietnam don't. Hannah didn't until she started dating Bob."

The judge's grass-cutting business must be good, I thought, if Bob had cash to play sugar daddy and buy antique clothing at silent auctions. "Do you know why Bob would buy a Chinese ceremonial robe?"

"Yeah, he bought it for Hannah. She was into that."

"How's that?"

She laughed. "Hannah wanted to wear it on special occasions." She made the word *special* sound like sex.

"He paid eight thousand dollars for the robe."

The sarcastic smile again. "Very special occasions."

"He sounds like a nice boyfriend."

"Not nice. Rich. Can't blame Hannah, though. I lived in a fancy place, too, for a couple months, and he bought me expensive clothes. We ate at good restaurants. He liked to screw at cheap motels, though. He used to take me to a place on Superior that cost about thirty bucks a night. You couldn't count on clean sheets."

Henry lighted a cigarette.

I said, "What's the connection to Charlie? He's an expert on Chinese robes, isn't he?"

Morell groaned as if he'd heard his name called from the bottom of the sea.

"Hannah met Bob at that auction. Charlie'd heard that the robe was being sold and took her with him, hoping to buy it—for himself, not her. He collects and studies those things. Anyway, Hannah saw Bob and liked what she saw, so she brushed up against him and told him what she would let him do to her if he bought the robe for her. It was a game, you know? She and Bob left the auction together—with the robe."

"Sounds like a nasty game."

She shrugged. "If a guy can't take a joke, fuck 'im, right?"

"Could Charlie take a joke?"

She glanced at Morell, sad and a little disgusted, the way you would look at a sick bird you thought you would have to bury. "Hannah ripped him up pretty bad."

"How bad?"

She thought about it; then her eyes got big. "Oh, no, not that bad. He wouldn't hurt anyone. I mean, what's he going to do? You saw him. He's nice, but he's a guy who dances by himself. And then passes out. That's Charlie."

I looked at Morell on the floor. The sweat on his bald head shined in the light. His braid fell around his neck like a noose. "How many hits of ecstasy did he do?"

She shrugged. "I saw him do four. He's pretty ripped up."

"You want to call the paramedics?"

She went to Morell, nudged him hard in the ribs with her toes. He groaned again. It was a groan of the living. She looked at me sideways. "What do you think?"

"He ever do this before?"

"Yeah, right in this spot."

"If he pukes, watch to make sure he doesn't choke on it."

She nodded as if she'd heard it before and probably done it. Then she returned to the couch and straddled Henry again. She pulled his shirt off his shoulders and bit him on the neck. He slid a hand back under her skirt.

"You got Hannah's apartment number at the Donatello Suites?" I asked.

"Twenty-three oh six," she mumbled, and she kissed Henry hard on the lips.

I went to the stereo cabinet and turned on the strobe light. The speaker wires hung out of the back of the tuner. If they wanted music, they would have to do their own electrical repairs.

FIFTEEN

A DOORMAN DRESSED IN khakis and a blue blazer stood at the entrance to the Donatello Suites lobby. The marble floor tile and the wood paneling on the walls looked like something you would find in a rich man's private library.

I walked past the doorman like I belonged, fished in my pockets for keys I didn't have, then followed a Japanese man through the door from the lobby to the elevators. The elevator bell sounded like a cash register: *Ding!* Twenty-third floor. You're a millionaire. The hall carpet was soft. They probably padded it with hundred-dollar bills.

I figured no one would be in Apartment 2306, but I knocked anyway. Silence. The door and the door frame were steel, and the top lock was a Medico. If it was locked, I wouldn't be able to pick it without more tools. But a lot of traffic had flowed through the door in the three and a half weeks since Le Thi Hanh died—police investigators, family members, building personnel—and after a while people get lazy. If someone broke in and stole the TV, who was going to complain? Not the tenant. I worked on the cheap bottom lock, and a minute later I was in.

The apartment had one bedroom, plus a living room/dining area and a small kitchen, hardwood floors throughout. The windows went from floor to ceiling. The furniture was purple and chrome, Hannah's idea of stylish living. Or maybe Bob's.

The place showed the marks of visitors before me: drawers and closet doors left an inch open, commercial cleaning supplies in the master bathroom. Someone had swept everything, including the toothpaste, out of the medicine cabinet. Probably cops with evidence bags. The cabinet beneath the sink was empty, too.

The bedroom windows had no shades, and a telescope pointed into another apartment tower a couple hundred yards away. People watching Hannah from the other building would see the telescope facing them. The top dresser drawer had jewelry, some of it nice, most of it in store boxes. Gifts from Bob probably. The next three drawers contained underwear, bras, pajamas, and exercise clothes. The bottom drawer had more tools than my toolbox, and you couldn't fix a broken chair with any of them. But you wouldn't want to massage your lover's body with the tools in my toolbox.

The walk-in closet was stuffed with dresses, skirts, and pants. In the middle of one of the racks was the blue Chinese robe from the silent auction picture. Its silk shined with a blue you find only in things that people don't make, and the animals on the sleeves looked fiercer than any thug I'd ever faced. I understood why someone would pay eight thousand dollars for the robe. I took it off the hanger and brought it into the bedroom, put it on Hannah's bed. You didn't go to dinner parties in a robe like this; you hung a robe like this on a museum wall and charged people to see it.

But when I spread it out, a shiver started up my neck. The middle of the robe split open into wide ribbons. Someone had cut it. And they hadn't done a neat job of it. They had slashed it four times across the front.

I went back into the closet and pulled the fanciest dress from the rack, spread it out against the other clothes. It was slashed, too. I dropped the dress on the floor and pulled down another. Slashed. Nine of the dresses and blouses were cut into shreds.

I turned off the closet light and walked into the living room. Why would someone destroy Hannah's clothes? Would Morell have sliced the robe after Hannah played her vicious game with him? Would he also have sliced her neck in the airport Hilton?

I went to the window. To the southeast, past one end of the facing apartment building, a band shell rose into the air in Millennium Park. Beyond the park, sailboats swung on their moorings in Monroe Harbor. To the northeast, the underbelly of storm clouds hung far out over the lake.

Who else would have slashed Le Thi Hanh's clothes? Chinh liked knives, and he hadn't approved of the life his sister was living. He could have cut the clothes to send her a message. But he wouldn't have done that after she died, and if he'd done it before, why would she have kept the slashed clothes with her other dresses?

The sound of a key in the door broke my thought. I slipped into the kitchen and hung close to the wall, slid my Glock out of its holster.

The door opened and a tall black man came in. His head jutted forward like a waterbird's. Mr. and Mrs. Le's neighbor in Little Vietnam. He propped the door open, then wandered through the living room and into the bedroom.

A dresser drawer opened and then rattled as the old man removed it. Several seconds later, he passed the kitchen carrying the drawer—the bottom one, full of sex toys—and disappeared out the door. After a minute, he returned. The drawer was empty. He went back into the bedroom.

When he came out again, he carried the blue ceremonial robe that I'd left on the bed and the slashed clothes I'd dropped on the closet floor. Before he got to the front door, I stepped out of the kitchen behind him, my Glock pointed at the small of his long back.

"Where are you going with that, old man?" I said.

He dropped the clothes and sprinted out the door. He was fast for an old man. But by the time he got to the door to the fire well, I had my gun pressed to his ear. I marched him back down the hall to Hannah's apartment and closed the door, then pushed him toward the living room couch and told him to sit down.

I stood over him and told him to give me his wallet. His driver's license said his name was Jake Sanders, and he was seventy-one years old. It listed an address next door to Hannah's parents. The wallet also contained a card that identified Sanders for veteran's benefits, a picture of a little girl—a granddaughter or great-granddaughter—and about twenty dollars in cash.

I put my gun back in my rig and pointed my thumb at the pile of clothes by the front door. "Where were you taking all that?"

"Garbage chute down the hall. Throwing it out."

"Why would you want to do that?"

"Mr. and Mrs. Le asked me to. They saw this stuff when they came downtown after Hanh died. You know, you don't want to think of your kid this way. They called me last night from New Jersey and said they're coming back. So they gave me a list of things they didn't ever want to see again and asked me to clean the place up."

"So you're their house security and also their garbageman?"

"No." He looked at me as if I were too small to understand. "Just a friend. How about you? What're you doing hanging around in Hanh's apartment?"

"Just waiting for you. Why'd they ask you to get rid of the sliced-up clothes?"

"Who's going to wear them?"

"The robe is worth eight thousand dollars."

He shook his head. "Not to me. Looks like rags."

"What else is on the garbage list?"

"Some magazines. And some self-portraits. Solo stuff. Not the kind of thing you want the neighbors to see." He smiled the littlest smile. "Except me, of course."

"Yeah. You seem real close to Hannah's parents. I

would've thought they would ask their sons to clean the apartment."

"Did you meet the boys?"

"Chinh held a knife to my throat, and the two of them followed me around the city for a day, if that's what you call 'meeting.'"

He nodded. "If you had a job like this, would you want them to do it or me?"

"I don't know. I don't know you yet. How did you get into the apartment?"

He reached into his pocket and pulled out a single key. "Building manager gave it to Mr. and Mrs. Le. They told me where to find it in their house."

"And why'd you run from me?"

"Hell, a man comes at you with a gun, you going to stop and talk about the horse races?"

"Okay," I said.

He nodded, like it was all settled, then started to get up from the couch.

"Sit down." I stepped toward him. I figured he was being straight with me, but I would knock him down if I needed to. He relaxed back into the cushions, as if he had all day. "I want a couple things from you. When you leave, I want you to take the clothes with you. Don't throw them out, and don't leave them here for her parents to throw out. The magazines and snapshots you can get rid of if you want."

He nodded. "You're sure excited about the clothes."

"And I want the parents' phone number in New Jersey. Your number, too."

"Why you want mine?"

I winked at him. "You're a good-looking man, Mr. Sanders."

He narrowed his eyes. "Just give me the damn paper and pen."

I had none, so I went into the kitchen and tried the drawers. In the third one, I found a stack of notepads and a bunch of loose pens. I grabbed what I needed and went back into the living room, but then stopped hard. I sat down on the couch next to him. The pad was the kind that hotels leave in the rooms for guests to scribble on and take with them when they leave. The hotel name was printed across the top. It said O'HARE HILTON. The pad in Hannah's kitchen drawer meant she'd gone to the hotel before the night of the murder. And that might mean the murder was part of something bigger than a one-night fit of jealousy or rage.

I handed the pad to Jake Sanders, and he noticed, too. "Jesus. Isn't this where Hanh died?"

I went back into the kitchen and opened the drawer. There were five more O'Hare Hilton pads. I took them into the living room and tossed them next to Sanders on the couch.

"Wow," he shook his head. "Pretty weird. What's it mean?"

I figured it meant Hannah was a regular customer at the O'Hare Hilton. It was Hannah's hotel, not the hotel of the mystery couple who'd left Club 9 with her. The blood trail ran from the Hilton room to who knew where. I said, "Hell if I know what it means."

He shook his head some more. "You going to search the apartment?"

"No," I said. "I'm done with that."

He looked a little disappointed. "What are you going to do?"

"I'm going to the O'Hare Hilton."

He hesitated. "You want me to ride along?"

He seemed like a good man, a man I wanted for a friend at times like this. "Thanks, but no."

He handed me a sheet of Hilton paper with two phone numbers. "Well, you can call me if you want to." He stood up. There was a chest and some bookshelves on the other side of the room. He went to the chest and opened it. The drawer was full of the magazines Hannah's parents had asked him to throw out. "Man," he said, "you gotta be careful what you leave in your drawers when you die."

SIXTEEN

THE CITY STREETS WERE thick with mid-afternoon traffic. In another hour, suits and dresses would pour out of the office buildings and everyone would sit in cars and wait for the jam to break and release them to whatever happiness or sadness was expecting them at home. This evening when I went home, I would find Jason waiting for me. If I had time, I would pick up some ice cream; we would sit after dinner and talk about how he liked school.

I drove to Congress Parkway and out of the Loop. At the junction of the Eisenhower Expressway and the Kennedy, I felt a tug toward the western suburbs, where Bill was lying in a hospital room. If I took the Eisenhower, I could be by his side in twenty minutes. I could sit with Eileen and Annie and wait for good news or bad. I could be part of it.

But I took the lanes onto the Kennedy Expressway and drove toward the airport. Instead of holding Bill's hand as he danced between the living and the dead, I called his room on my cell phone.

Annie answered. "Dad's in and out of consciousness," she said. "They're treating the infection aggressively, and his fever's down, so the doctors are optimistic."

"Good. And how are you doing?"

"I'm doing all right. Optimistic, too." But she sounded like she'd been crying.

"I'll drop by tomorrow," I said. I hadn't seen her since she graduated from high school, first in her class and heading off for an accelerated premed program. Bill's smile that day was bigger than I'd ever seen.

Next, I called my office for messages. Ben Turner had called to ask me to phone him about a problem with Bob Piedras. The problem probably meant more boxes of telephone records for me, so I deleted the message.

A woman named Sandra Peterson had called to find out if I did employee theft and loss prevention. I did, so I saved the message.

The last message was from Corrine, who said, "I was thinking about what you said about quitting your job and moving. Do you really think sex on a boat would give me multiple orgasms?"

I grinned. The first time I dialed her number, my thumb hit all the wrong buttons. The second time, her answering machine picked up. I said, "If a motorboat doesn't do it, we'll try a sailboat. If a sailboat doesn't do it, we'll try a canoe. If it floats, we'll try it." I wanted to tell her I loved her, but I couldn't go there. Not yet. Instead, I told her I would call again.

Twenty minutes later, I pulled into short-term parking at O'Hare Airport. The Hilton was located in the middle of the airport's four terminals. When George Jetson visited Chicago, he could ride the moving sidewalk to the hotel from parking, listening to space-age music and watching a long neon sculpture above him. Me, I walked.

The Hilton check-in desk was about as long as a tavern bar. If you added stools, dressed the clerks in jeans, and put liquor bottles where the international monetary exchange rates were posted, you could open for business. I waited in line until a thin clerk with a name badge that identified him as Philip beckoned me with his index finger. He put on a smarmy smile when he welcomed me to the Hilton and asked how he could help me.

I asked if the night manager was available.

He made a show of lifting his wrist and looking at his watch skeptically. "It's just four-fifteen." But he went into a room behind the counter, and a moment later the night manager came out. She was a dark-haired woman in her late twenties, wearing a short blue skirt and a matching jacket. Her tan said she spent her off-duty hours sleeping in the sun.

"My name is Cynthia Nichols," she said with the same smile as the clerk's. "How can I help you?"

I flashed my detective's license and told her I was investigating Le Thi Hanh's death.

"Of course," she said, as if she'd been expecting me. She led me around the counter and into an office. She closed the door and sat behind a desk. "I'm supposed to send you to our PR guy, but if I do that, he'll call legal, and legal will meet for a week, and then they'll set up a time for the five of us to get together: you, me, the PR guy, and two lawyers."

"I appreciate your talking to me."

"It's easier this way. If I went through the whole process every time we had a problem like this, I'd never get my work done."

"You have a lot of problems like this?"

"We have eight hundred and fifty-eight guest rooms. It's a rare night when we don't call the police for something or other."

"For a murder?"

She laced her manicured fingers on the desk. "No, that doesn't happen often."

"Do the police have all the video of the couple and Le Thi Hanh?"

She lost a battle against fidgeting, reached into a desk drawer for a pack of Newports, lighted one, and inhaled as if it were oxygen and she'd spent a long time underwater. "They have everything from the night of the murder."

"Do you archive old security video?"

She shook her head no, exhaled.

"I think Le Thi Hanh might have stayed here a few times recently," I said.

"Oh, I don't think so, though I can check the computer." She typed on the keyboard. "Most of our return customers are business travelers from out of town. They stay here so they can catch early-morning flights." She stared at the monitor. "Well, this time I'm wrong.

Le Thi Hanh registered as a guest three times in the last six months: in April, July, and August. The night of her murder, she was in the room of other registered guests."

"That probably happened more than once."

"We can't get information about that kind of visit, of course." But she turned back to her monitor and read. "This is surprising. Like the couple she was with, she requested a room on the seventh floor each time."

"What's special about the seventh floor?"

"Nothing, except it's the one floor we haven't renovated."

"Any reason why people ask for unrenovated rooms? Cheaper?"

"Same price. My guess is the mirrors."

"The mirrors?"

"Facing the bed. The old rooms had them; the new ones don't."

Hannah liked to watch others watching her. "Could I see the room where she was killed?"

She frowned. "We're using the room again, since the police have finished with it, but let me see." Again she typed on the keyboard. "You're in luck, if that's the right word for it. The room is empty this afternoon."

She got keys from the front desk and we rode the elevator to the seventh floor.

The room was a standard mid-range, high-volume one. The queen-size bed had a cover so slick with Scotch Guard, you could have slid a cracked egg across it. Like the night manager had promised, a large wall mirror faced the bed. Beside the mirror, an Impressionist print was bolted to the wall, as if people willing to stuff it into their suitcase and take it home didn't deserve to look at a little boy in an oxcart for the rest of their lives.

The window looked out at the airport. Enormous planes lifted off, noses to the sky, and disappeared into the low clouds, seeming to break every physical law that kept big things solidly on the ground. The hotel had invested in good soundproofing, and the planes were as quiet as birds lifting into the air from a pond. Someone could scream in a room like this, and no one would ever hear. Did Hannah come out of her drugged-up dreams and scream as the knife slashed at her throat? I wondered, Did she know she was screaming inside a can?

I asked, "On the night of the killing, did any of the other guests report a disturbance from the room?"

"No," said the night manager sadly. "No one. But most of the guests here pay very little attention to one another. Most of them stay only one night, and they come and go at all hours. They arrive after delayed flights in the middle of the night and then check out at four in the afternoon. Or four in the morning."

"That's probably why Le Thi Hanh chose to stay here. No one would be surprised when she walked through the lobby at three A.M., or when she walked back out a couple hours later. Or maybe she just came for the mirrors."

The night manager smiled at herself in the mirror. "I guess they're nice, if you like that kind of thing."

I walked back to the parking garage alone. My car was on the third floor, wedged between a couple of SUVs. If VW Bugs had been parked next to me, I might have seen Chinh and Lanh coming. Or if I were an NBA center. But VW bugs weren't parked next to me, and I'm six one, a little taller in my shoes. I didn't even sense Chinh and Lanh until they were right behind me. I spun. I don't know how far I got. Something hit me on the head and I went down. I opened my eyes as the Le brothers dragged me across the parking lot and put me in the backseat of their car. Lanh drove, and Chinh sat beside me with his knife in his hand. Not that he needed it. I think I tried to say something smart to him, but the words got tangled in my mouth. I remember the dull sunlight flashing through the car windows as we rolled out of the parking garage. Then nothing.

SEVENTEEN

WHEN I WOKE, IT was dark except for the light of a
TV. My head hurt, the kind of hurt that makes you want
to close your eyes and caress your temples with your
thumbs. But that wouldn't work. My hands were cuffed
to two corners of a bed frame. My feet were tied. No
use complaining about it—I had a gag in my mouth.

The TV was on to the ten o'clock news, medium loud,
loud enough to muffle gagged grunts, loud enough to
make my head pound. The weatherman was saying another cold front would blow into the city in the next
forty-eight hours. "More stormy weather," he said. "If
you want to go to the beach this weekend, you'd better
book tickets for Miami." Good advice, but too late.

The TV was fastened to the wall. That meant I was in
a motel room. The bed smelled like sweat and cigarette
smoke. The furniture was cheap. The curtain was heavy,
pulled closed. In the blue television light, a mosquito

skipped along the ceiling. Probably plotting what part of me to suck blood from.

The room looked like it hadn't had maid service in weeks. Chinh and Lanh probably paid by the month. Maybe they wouldn't come back until October. It was 10:30, and Lucinda was supposed to be at my house with videos from BlackLite. Jason probably was sitting on the living room floor again, hating me for abandoning him. I didn't think the two of them would arrange a search and rescue mission. Maybe when people finally came to the motel room, all they would find would be dried skin and bones and a very fat mosquito.

But then the door opened and Chinh and Lanh walked in. Lanh flipped on the light switch and turned off the TV. He had a bag of McDonald's takeout. Chinh's knife hung from his belt in a sheath. His face was bruised and his nose was swollen, probably broken. I figured Ben Turner's security team must have taken the Le brothers off my tail at the judge's house with their fists. I hated Turner a little more for it. Lanh had no marks on him, though.

Lanh sat in a chair next to the bed and ate a pack of Chicken McNuggets. Then he pulled the gag out of my mouth and dropped it on the floor. "Where's Bob Piedras?" he said. The question made me happy because it meant they probably weren't going to kill me or even hurt me too bad. This wasn't about me; they wanted Bob.

I worked my mouth muscles and tongue into shape and said, "Could I have a chicken nugget?" Lanh smacked me in the jaw with an open hand. It hurt enough to make me talk nice. I said, "I'll tell you what I know if you'll tell me something."

He looked impatient. Chinh did, too. He stood at the foot of the bed, fingering the knife. "What?" Lanh asked.

"Did Jake Sanders tell you that you could find me at the Hilton?"

"Why do you want to know?"

"I just want to know who my friends are."

"Yeah, Jake called. He said you broke into Hanh's apartment. He said you seemed like a nice guy, but he wonders why you would do that. So do I."

"I'm looking for Hanh's killer."

"Old story, and it's boring. Where's Piedras?"

I looked at Chinh. "Did that happen to your face out at the Dunes?"

He sneered. One of his front teeth was missing. "Did what happen?"

"Did a couple of boys in suits give you the make-over?"

He shrugged, but he also took the knife out of the sheath.

Lanh leaned in. "Where's Piedras?"

"I figured that was why you followed me. You hoped I would lead you to him."

"And we figured that's why you never met up with him."

"No," I said, "I tried to catch up with him in the Dunes. I was curious to see what would happen when you ran into each other."

"Where is he?"

"I don't think Bob did it. I think Chinh did."

Chinh came around the side of the bed, waving the knife. "I'm going to cut him."

"Who killed her, then?" I said. "And why?"

Before Chinh could answer, Lanh smacked my jaw again. He nodded at my neck, and Chinh calmly hung his knife over me, holding it between his thumb and forefinger. Lanh asked, "Where is he?"

"His lawyer's got him in hiding. The guys who broke Chinh's nose run security for the lawyer. They won't tell me, either."

"Who's the lawyer?" he said.

"Donald Sanke. He's a big-shot criminal lawyer. If you try to intimidate him, you'd better bring along some buddies."

Chinh sneered, but Lanh said, "I've heard of the guy." You could see him doing the arithmetic, figuring his chances against Sanke.

"You know," I said to Chinh, "if you drop that knife, it will cut my throat the same way the knife cut your sister's. Same size knife, too, from what forensics tells me."

"You're a stupid fuck."

"Anyone can see you loved your sister. No jury's going to believe it was premeditated. An accident, a slip of the fingers. That's the way they'll see it. You're not looking at the death penalty, or even life in prison. I give it twenty years max. If you can swing a lawyer like Donald Sanke, you might even walk out of jail in ten."

Chinh gripped the knife more firmly and turned to his brother. "Do you mind if I kill him?"

Lanh said, "Shut up."

"Yeah," I said, "shut up."

"Both of you. You know Chinh will cut you if you don't tell us where Piedras is."

"I told you already. I don't know where he is."

"That's too bad," he said, "because we need to find out if you're telling the truth."

Chinh flashed a big smile. He put the knife in the sheath, then punched me three times in the gut. He was a skinny guy, but he seemed to have done this kind of thing before, and after the third punch, tears ran from my eyes.

"Where's Piedras?" Lanh asked.

"I don't know," I said.

Chinh punched three more times in the same spot, like he was tenderizing meat.

"Where's Piedras?" Lanh asked again.

"How do you know he killed your sister?"

The fist hit me again, three more times. It knocked the breath out of me, and the room went black.

Then, a cold, wet cloth was wiping my face, my eyes, and I saw light and faces through a blur of sweat and tears. Lanh hovered over me. He looked perfectly calm. "Chinh hit you nine times," he said. "If he gets to ten, he uses the knife and starts digging. A layer at a time. Slow, you know? As long as it takes." He winked at me. "Do you understand?"

I think I said I did.

"It will hurt a lot more than anything you've ever felt before. You understand that, too?"

I must have said yes.

"Where is Piedras?" he asked again.

I lied. "You missed him at the Dunes." "He was inside, staying away from the windows." Fear of death didn't make me lie. Fear of not dying as the pain grew worse did. Nothing I could do but lie and feel like a coward for doing it. "Sanke's keeping him across the state line to slow down the process if he gets indicted."

They looked at each other as if they doubted it, but Chinh put the gag back in my mouth, and Lanh turned the TV up loud enough so no one would hear my grunts. Then he went to the bathroom and brought back a towel and wiped down my face again. He said, "If we don't find Piedras at the house, we'll come back and start again, but this time we go right to the knife." He turned off the light, and then they left.

I stayed there listening to David Letterman crack jokes. In less than an hour, Lanh and Chinh would surprise the judge. In two hours plus change, they would come back to do surgery on my kidneys because they'd discovered Bob wasn't there.

The cuffs cut into my wrists and were locked to a metal bed frame. Clothesline bound my feet. A phone stood on the dresser, but the dresser was miles away. I pulled against the cuffs until I lost feeling in my hands. All I could do was wait and hope Ben Turner and his security team already were at the judge's house and were used to attacks like the one Chinh and Lanh would spring on them. Twenty minutes passed, thirty. I thought of Jason alone at my house again, and how I was failing him. I thought of Kevin Morales dead on his mother's kitchen floor.

It was my fault.

It wasn't my fault.

It was and wasn't my fault. I'd never said his name to anyone after he died. Not to Mom and Dad. Not to the counselors who helped me break my bad habits, most of them.

Tears filled my eyes. Angry, sad tears; tears I'd fought back a thousand times. Now I didn't fight them. I lifted my body above the mattress and slammed it down. The metal bed frame smashed against the wall. I lifted my body again, slammed it down again. And again. I pounded my body against the bed as if it could absorb all the pain I'd caused, all the pain I felt.

On the fifth slam, someone yelled, "Quiet!" I pounded the bed again and the bed smacked the wall so hard that plaster snowed down on me. If I could bring down the ceiling, I figured I would do it. Two more smacks got a fist pounding on the other side of the wall.

After about five minutes, someone knocked at the door and yelled, "Manager!" I kept pounding, but now the anger and sadness lifted and I was laughing. It hurt my gutlike hell, but I was laughing. A small, thin-haired man wearing wire-rimmed glasses opened the door and flipped on the light. An old woman in a maid's uniform peered into the room from behind him. They looked at me like I was crazy. The man took a slow tour around the bed, inspecting me from every angle. He stopped near the head of the bed and peered down at me. "What I want to know is what the fuck you're doing in my motel." He checked to see that my hands were locked tight, then glanced back at the old woman at the door.

"If he moves, you run and call the cops." The woman nodded. He pulled the gag out of my mouth and said, "Tell me why I shouldn't call the cops."

I worked my mouth and calmed down. "Call the cops if you want. I'll give you the name of a couple of them who will thank you for the call. But if you want to keep the cops out of this, you can check my ID; and if you figure I'm okay when you see that I'm a private detective, you can find a way to get me out of the handcuffs."

He reached into my pocket, keeping his eyes on mine, then thumbed through the contents of my wallet. He spent a long time reading my license. Then he removed the three twenties and the five I was carrying and stuffed them in his pocket. "For the damage you did to the wall," he said. He threw the wallet next to me on the bed and left the room.

He came back a few minutes later with a small saw. "This'll cut through galvanized pipe," he said. "I don't know about handcuffs." He peeled off his T-shirt and put it on the dresser. He stopped short and said, "Is this a fucking joke?" He turned, lifting a key ring with two small keys off the top of the dresser.

I laughed again. I couldn't help it.

"If you knew these were here, I'll leave you to rot. I swear to God I will. I don't like to be fucked with."

I caught my breath. "I didn't know. I didn't see them. I couldn't. I've got a golf ball on the back of my head that says I was unconscious when they tied me up."

He came to the bed and unlocked my wrists. "Untie your fucking legs yourself."

As soon as I got free of the clothesline, I went to the

phone and called the judge. It rang four times before his answering machine picked up. I didn't bother with the details: "Two guys are heading your way looking for Bob. One of them has a knife; don't know what else they might be carrying. Turner can handle them easy as long as he sees them coming."

I found my Glock on a pile of blankets in the closet and saw the motel address stamped on a card on the back of the door. Since I figured I would have a hard time convincing the motel manager to lend me one of my twenties for cab fare, I called Corrine for another ride. She answered on the third ring. She sounded like she was sleeping, but she also seemed glad I'd called. I told her I'd had some more trouble and gave her an address in the 1400 block of Lawrence Avenue.

I walked outside and breathed deep in the city night. The pain in my gut made me retch, but I kept everything down. I spit, then tried breathing again, in and out, nice and easy. Up and down the street, the storefronts were dark. I looked into the sky. The moon was full and white and looked like it had a gardenia painted on it. But I knew if you got close enough, it would smell like dust and death.

EIGHTEEN

LAST THING I WANTED to talk about with Corrine was Chinh and Lanh. I didn't want to talk about the judge or Bob or Le Thi Hanh, either. Or why I was bumming a ride home from the Palm Court Motel at 11:30 at night. I wanted to talk about the Atlantic coast and the Gulf Coast, about the Cuban rhythms of Miami and a little shrimping village I'd heard about just south of the Georgia border.

But Corrine needed an explanation. When we were married, I didn't explain enough. So now more than ever, I needed to explain.

I told her about Hannah's murder in the Hilton, and she said, "Jesus, that's horrible."

"It gets worse. The cops think a guy I knew as a kid did it. Judge Rifkin called me a couple—"

"You're talking to the judge again?"

"He asked me to try to clear my friend."

"You said you'd never talk to him again."

"I still feel like I owe him something. I don't know why."

"That's crazy."

So much for the value of explaining.

"You think your friend killed her?"

"Maybe."

Talking wasn't making either of us feel better, so I gave a quick version of how the Le brothers had knocked me out and played bongos on my kidneys; then I shut up, and we drove toward my house, listening to the tires on the pavement.

The night was warm, but a rough wind had started blowing again, kicking up dust and garbage. We stopped at a red light. A plastic grocery bag blew across the street and flew up the side of an apartment building. A couple of guys crossed from another corner, hunched against the warm wind the way they would hunch all winter against the cold. A pawnshop's yellow sign glowed on one corner, and on another the icy lights of a twenty-four-hour gas station were shining. Down the street, a liquor store was open. But the night felt dark. Even in the dismal orange streetlights, even under the full moon, the night felt dark.

"I'm going to drop you off and get myself home, all right?" Corrine spoke to the windshield.

"Long day?"

She shrugged. "New client. They live in a penthouse on Lake Shore Drive. Thirty-fourth floor. I spent the afternoon in their patio garden, taking out the summer planting and putting in fall flowers. A thousand dollars' worth of zinnias. They have vines on trellises hanging over the side of the building; I trimmed those. Other than that, it was a normal job. I mulched a bunch of planters."

Even on top of thirty-four stories of concrete, things grew. Corrine touched them and they bloomed. I sat next to her and listened, and I felt like if I had her touch again, I could live better, too. I didn't expect any fancy blooms, and I probably wouldn't grow, but at least I could live better.

I put my hand on her thigh and felt her warmth through her jeans. She didn't tell me to take my hand off, so I left it there and we drove the rest of the way, quiet again, both of us watching the street in front of us.

When we pulled to the curb outside my house, she turned off the motor. She looked at me, waited for me to make the next move. "Were you serious in your phone message?" I asked. "Are you willing to try again?"

She pushed a strand of hair behind her ear with her thumb. "It depends on what you mean by 'try again.'"

"I don't know. The whole thing, I suppose. Share a house. Share a bed. Talk. Fight now and then. You know, live a life together."

"That's a lot," she said. "I don't know if I'm ready for something that big again."

"We're that big. I know we are. Trust me. Trust us."

"Trust," she said softly, like it was something only fools did. "You know, there're some guys who surf the easy waves through life. Everything's a ride. If they have a good business lunch or sell an insurance policy, they're pumped up. If they take a spill, they get up and try again. Those guys are easy to live with. They're easy to be around." In the streetlight, her eyes glistened.

"You're not one of those guys. You're one of the other guys, the ones who are bored with regular life. They want danger. They're not easy to live with. That's you, Joe. Do you understand what I'm saying?"

"Since when do you surf?" I asked.

She gave me a tight-lipped smile. "It's a metaphor."

"You dating someone who surfs?"

"This isn't about me."

"I love you," I said. "I don't know about surfing. I know you're probably right about me. But I also know that you're my biggest thrill."

The exasperated smile turned into something warmer.

"What do you want?" I asked. "Do you want to have a family? Do you want—"

She put a finger to my lips, then leaned in and kissed me. We stayed like that awhile before she pulled away. "I do miss you," she said.

"I want to know what I can do to make you happy."

"Let's start slow and easy, okay?" she whispered. "I want you to make love to me tonight."

"You do?"

"You see? Easy. Nothing difficult."

I thought about that. "Easy sex? Tomorrow you just wake up and drive away?"

"I didn't say that."

I nodded slowly. "Good. Then come inside."

We stood in the living room and kissed. My hands explored her. Her shoulders, the bone that lifted in the skin just below her neck. Her back, the curve down and in, the rhythm of her ribs. The soft flesh as I moved down.

Then her lips pulled away from mine and she screamed.

"What?" I shouted.

She pointed at the kitchen doorway. Jason stood there in his Batman pajamas. His mask was on. The pointy bat ears stood out to the sides. He was using a knuckle to wipe sleep from an eye through a bat eyehole.

"What is that?" Corrine said.

"It's an eleven-year-old boy," I said. "His name is Jason."

"When did you have a child?"

"He's my cousin. He's visiting from Miami."

She did some slow calculations. "Is this why you're asking me about starting a family?"

"Huh?"

"The boy. Jason. Your cousin. Do you want me back because you're taking care of him now?"

"No. Jason has nothing to do with it. Trust me."

"Trust you? You didn't tell me you've got a goddamn kid living with you."

"I'm taking care of him. He's staying here awhile."

Jason pointed at Corrine, accusing her. "Is she your girlfriend?"

"She's my ex-wife."

He looked at us suspiciously, like he knew something about adult relationships that we hadn't figured out yet.

Corrine eyed me suspiciously, too. "I don't get it, Joe."

I gave her my open palms. "What's there to get?"

Her eyes glittered with tears. "What was supposed to happen in the morning? Was Batman going to come to your bedroom with breakfast on a tray? Is that the way you surprise me with the news that you've got a kid living with you?"

Jason scratched his head through the mask, twisting one of the ears upright. "Is she always this nutty?"

"Take off the mask," I said. "And she's not nutty. She's upset."

"Damn right I'm upset." She started toward the door.

"Please stay." I knew better than to go after her and try to hold her.

"I can't do this, Joe. I can't." And she was outside.

Jason and I stood in the living room and watched her go. We listened to her start her car and pull away. Jason said, "She's nutty."

I spun on him. "Take off that damn mask."

He shrugged and did.

I wanted bourbon. On the rocks in a tall glass. Skip the rocks if there was no ice. Skip the glass if there was no glass. Nights like this were why counselors made drunks like me pour every bottle down the drain, keeping nothing in the house for guests. I would have driven out to a store for a bottle, except my car was still in short-term parking at the airport. I would have called a cab, except I was too beaten to do it. So we sat at the kitchen table, drinking milk and eating *bigos* stew cold from the pot Mom had left in the fridge.

After a while, I said, "I'm sorry I wasn't here tonight."

"It doesn't matter." Jason kept his eyes on his bowl.

"It does matter. I wanted to be here. I tried to—"

"I don't care."

I sat back in my chair. "Giving up on me?"

He shrugged.

"I had some trouble from the Vietnamese men you met yesterday."

The smallest glimmer of interest. "Did Chinh pull the knife on you again?"

"For a starter, yeah."

He ate a bite of *bigos*.

I leaned back in my chair. "How was school?"

"Fine."

"You like your teacher?"

"She's fine."

"You make any new friends?"

Eyes on the bowl. "Why bother? I'm leaving in a couple weeks."

"You should bother because this is where you are now." Advice from the untrustworthy.

When he finished his *bigos*, I said, "Did a woman named Lucinda Juarez come by or call?"

He looked up from his bowl for the first time. "Yeah. Around ten-thirty. She got me into bed." He glanced at me. "I like her."

"Yeah, I like her, too."

"Is *she* your girlfriend?"

"No, she's a cop," I said, as if that explained something. "Did she say how I could reach her?"

"She said she would come by again in a couple hours."

A couple hours was now, so I wasn't surprised when she knocked a few minutes later and walked in with a box of DVDs.

She handed me the box and went to Jason, ruffled his matted hair. "Hey, why are you still awake?"

He gave her a grin to melt hearts. "Because you said you were coming back."

Lucinda turned to me. "Doesn't he have school tomorrow?"

I nodded. "At eight-thirty."

"Then come on," she said, and she took Jason by the hand and the three of us walked down the hall to his room. He climbed into bed, glanced at me nervously, then put on his Batman mask again.

Lucinda tucked his covers around him and reached for the light.

He said, "Will you give me a kiss?" An eleven-year-old on the make.

She smiled and kissed him on the cheek, just below the mask. He kissed her on the cheek, too. He looked at me like he expected something, so I kissed his forehead, between the bat ears.

"What a great kid," Lucinda said when we got back to the living room.

"Yeah, but he's going to kill himself sleeping in that mask."

"That's not what's going to kill him."

That stopped me short. I looked at her for the rest.

"You don't leave a kid that age at home without an adult."

I didn't bother telling her about banging the motel bed against the wall so I could get home to Jason. When you added it all up, it was a lame excuse. "He's used to it."

"Yeah, all the more reason you don't do it."

I said, "Let's watch a movie."

But she looked me up and down. "Are you all right?"

"Yeah, I'm fine. Sorry I was late."

She didn't look convinced. "You know, Joe, you're a smart guy. I know you are. And I know you've got feelings. Why else would you do this work? But I've never in my life met anyone so . . . insulated. You're hard on the outside, but I can't believe you're hard on the inside."

"Actually, I'm crunchy on the outside, chewy in the middle."

"You're a bastard. This is exactly what I mean."

"I'm sorry," I said.

"No you aren't."

"I am. Really. I'm just not ready to talk about this right now."

She sighed. "You tell me when you're ready."

I nodded. "Let's watch a movie, okay?"

She sighed again, but she opened the box and pulled out three DVDs, leaving five more. "I've watched about twenty videos, and the rough cuts look promising. In one of them, the director walks into the shot, but you never see his face. In a couple, you hear the director's voice. But mostly it's just a lot of sex scenes." She read the handwritten titles on the cases. "What's your mood? *Passion Fruit*, *Everything Butt*, or *Forbidden Pleasures*?"

I shrugged. "*Passion Fruit*."

She put it in the player, and we settled down together on the couch.

A big-breasted blonde was making dinner in a kitchen. She had on a short cotton skirt and a blouse that hung open and revealed everything but nipple. A dinner table was set for six in the background: candles, wineglasses, formal place settings. The woman was cooking for a party. She poured a glass of wine while she cooked, and she caressed the bottle neck. She drank straight and long from the bottle. A single drop of wine ran down her chin, down her neck, between her breasts.

She opened the fridge and leaned over the vegetable drawer. She had nothing on under her skirt.

"Why is she cooking without panties on?" Lucinda asked.

"Hot in the kitchen."

She pulled green beans out of the drawer. They weren't what she was looking for. She pulled out a mango. She rubbed it against her cheek, down her neck, between her breasts. Her blouse fell open. She caressed her body with the mango, then lifted her skirt and rubbed the mango between her legs.

She did the same thing with a pear. Then a cucumber, same thing, but when she rubbed it between her legs, she put it inside her.

"Man, that's got to be cold," Lucinda said.

The blonde sat on the floor, trying out all the fruits and vegetables—an apple, a zucchini, a carrot, an orange, two bananas. She pulled something long and hairy out of the vegetable keeper. It belonged on a rhinoceros, not in a vegetable keeper.

"What the hell is that?" I said.

"I think it's a yucca."

"It's obscene is what it is."

The guests arrived. The first was a black man with a

tight Afro. He had a six-pack of beer. He pulled out a bottle, opened it, drank some, inserted the neck of the bottle in the woman.

"No, that's not a good idea," Lucinda said.

After a while, three couples were going at it on the kitchen floor, on the butcher block, on the kitchen counter, in the sink. Two Yorkshire terriers in leather corsets ran into the kitchen and licked up the food the couples dropped on the floor. Maybe it was a joke. Maybe we're all just little dogs in leather corsets. We do ridiculous things with our bodies to give ourselves pleasure. The dogs looked like they were having as much fun as anyone else. The dinner table stayed in the background. Only the dogs ate.

We fast-forwarded through the rest of the DVD, slowing or stopping it when new actors came on or when a cut made us think we might hear or see something important.

Lucinda took the disc out of the player. "See anything?"

I shook my head. "But I learned more about the four basic food groups."

"It's my turn," she said, and she put a DVD into the machine. *Forbidden Pleasures* showed couples having sex in public places: in a park I didn't recognize, on an El platform I did, in an office. Lucinda didn't crack jokes about the video, and she didn't fast-forward it. I didn't, either. We sank into the couch cushions a couple inches apart, and I felt the danger before either of us said anything. But I didn't turn off the DVD.

Lucinda said, "If you weren't married—"

I thought about my talk with Corrine and my hopes that we would get back together. The video cut to a couple making love on a towel at the beach. "I'm not married," I said.

We watched some more. A woman was moaning on a picnic blanket in the woods.

"Ah, she's faking it," Lucinda said.

I shrugged. "Faking it is okay."

She glanced at me, raised her eyebrows.

"It is," I said. "You know, it's better than nothing."

She smiled and turned back to the video. "What the hell, then, right?" She put a hand on my knee, ran it slowly up the inside of my leg.

My leg muscles tensed.

She said, "Not ready for this, either?"

"I think I'm still with Corrine."

"She divorced you, Joe."

"I know."

She took her hand off my leg.

"I'm sorry," I said.

"Don't be," she replied, but I was anyway.

We sat on the couch and watched other couples enjoying their forbidden pleasures on my twenty-inch screen. My whole body was ringing with desire for Lucinda and I wondered if she could hear it.

We made it through the DVD and then popped in *Everything Butt*. It was as bad as *Passion Fruit*, and about halfway through, I fell asleep.

I dreamed to a sound track of love grunts and moans. They were happy dreams, some with Corrine, some with women I'd never seen before, but they loved me and I wanted them. Later, I dreamed I was fishing with Corrine. We wore swimsuits and were tan and young. The fishing boat was scrubbed white and it danced on glittering ocean waves. The light was almost blinding, but it felt warm and good. Jason came out onto the deck from the cabin, and he was happy and tan, too. We drifted on the ocean, happy to be fishing, happy to be together. Then a voice called out of the cabin, "Turn to the right!" It was the judge's voice, and I thought the boat was about to run into something—a buoy or a coral reef. I reached for a steering wheel that wasn't there, and the judge's voice called again, "Turn to the right!"

I woke. The judge's face stared at me, frozen on the television screen. His hands were holding someone's naked shoulders.

"What is this?" I said.

Lucinda smiled. "The director."

"The judge is the director?"

"Who the hell is the judge?"

"Oh shit," I said.

I told her about Judge Peter Rifkin and about Bob Piedras and Le Thi Hanh. When I talked with the judge the morning after Ahmed Hassan's killing, he said he had seen me on TV, and he asked me about Hassan's killing, what I saw, what I didn't, why I was there. Now I realized the judge was asking because he was connected to the killing.

We watched the scene again and again. The judge told an actress to turn right, but she turned left. The judge stepped into the picture and gripped her naked shoulders. He turned her the way he wanted her. "Turn to the right!" he ordered.

"Fuck you, Judge," I said to the screen.

"Why would he call you after Hassan's killing?" Lucinda asked.

"I don't know," I said. "He must have been looking to protect himself or someone else."

"Who?"

I thought about it. "Bob Piedras could've been the guy in the yellow hat. The judge knows I used to be friends with Bob, and if Bob was involved in Hassan's killing, he would've wondered why I was at the store. He couldn't find out without bringing me in."

"How does this tie into Le Thi Hanh getting her throat cut?"

"It might not. Do any of the videos you've seen feature Asian women?"

"Yeah, two or three of them." She pulled one called *Facets of Jade* out of her box. She put it in the player, and Le Thi Hanh appeared on the screen. She walked through an airport terminal, wearing a blue Chinese ceremonial robe. She walked toward the camera, staring at the lens.

The video cut to a hotel room. It could have been a room at the O'Hare Hilton or at a hotel like the Hilton. Three men came into the room. She let the robe fall off her shoulders. One by one, they had sex with her. She took them passively, never reacting to them at all; she let them do what they wanted to her. And she kept staring at the camera.

The men left and Hannah put on the robe again,

leaving it unfastened. A fourth man came into the hotel room. I knew the man. He carried a knife with a blade that had to be ten inches long. "Damn!" I said.

Lucinda said, "Bob Piedras?"

"The son of a bitch," I said.

Bob went to Hannah and held the knife at her throat. He traced a line from her neck down between her breasts to her belly, then down to her pubic hair. She pulled the robe closed. He raised the knife and slashed the cloth over her left breast, then the cloth over her right breast, but never broke skin, never drew blood. He slashed the cloth over each breast again and again, and she stood exposed.

He threw the knife down and took Hannah and lowered her to the floor. Then he had sex with her. This time, she wasn't passive. His hunger for her was huge, but hers for him was bigger. They never made a sound, but they gripped each other so hard, you could hear the howl inside them. And the whole time, Hannah never took her eyes off the camera. She watched us watching her.

"Jesus!" I said.

"Yeah, Jesus Christ," said Lucinda. "You know where Piedras is?"

"No." I looked at my watch. It was almost 5:00 A.M. Donald Sanke's law office would open in two or three hours. "But I can find out in the next couple of hours."

"What about the judge?"

"Yeah, I know where to find him."

Lucinda was up off the couch. "Let's go." But when she saw me hanging back, she slowed down. "You want to get the judge by yourself, don't you?"

I nodded. "The judge and I go back to when I was a kid. I've got to do this right." I knew I sounded like Chinh and Lanh saying they needed to handle their sister's murder themselves, but I didn't much care.

She sat down. "I want to be in on Piedras. If he shot Bill, I need to—"

I put my hand on hers. "We'll go after Piedras together. We both need that."

She settled into the couch. "Okay." She smiled, suddenly looking tired. "I'll get some sleep and then go into the station."

"When I talked with Bob, he said he had an assault charge against him from awhile back. It involved a woman he was dating."

"I'll see what I can dig up." She pointed her thumb toward Jason's room. "What are you going to do about Jason?"

"Damn," I said.

"You can't keep forgetting him."

"I know."

"Don't worry about it right now," she said. "I'll get him to school."

"You're a good friend."

She nodded. "Don't ever forget it."

"Will you do me one more favor?"

"What?"

"Can you lend me your car?"

She handed me the keys without asking why.

NINETEEN

I SPED TO THE Dunes in Lucinda's Civic and parked on the side of the road about fifty yards beyond the judge's driveway, then jogged back to his house.

The front door stood wide open. I stepped inside and called for the judge, but no one answered. I called again, louder, standing at the bottom of the stairs. No answer. I walked into the living room. It looked just like it had the day before. A picture of the judge hung on one of the walls, but there was no judge.

In the kitchen, the sun shined brightly through double French doors. You could let a slow morning slide away in a room like this, reading the newspaper and drinking coffee, looking out the window now and then to enjoy the light bouncing off the water of the swimming pool. On the kitchen table, half a cigar was propped on a butter plate. Half a dozen empty glasses stood on the counter next to the sink. One was speckled with dried orange juice pulp. The other five smelled like whiskey.

I looked out the window over the sink and saw the judge in the pool. "Bastard," I mumbled, and walked out the French doors to deal with him. The pool water rippled in the breeze. An irrigation sprinkler watered the climbing roses by the door to the pool house. The wind took the tops off the jets and the mist sparkled in the air. The judge floated on his back, face to the sun. Doctors would have told him that was the way to get skin cancer. But he was seventy-two years old and he had only a few more years to enjoy the world. If that meant smoking a cigar and risking mouth cancer, he would smoke. If it meant floating in his pool facing the sun, he would float in his pool facing the sun.

He floated, completely still. It was just about the perfect morning.

But in his forehead he had a bullet hole, washed pink by the chlorinated water.

My legs went soft when I saw the wound, and I sank down on the concrete. My eyes stung with tears. I sat a long time. "You bastard," I said, and I sat some more.

Then I coaxed his body to the pool edge with a net used to skim leaves out of the water. I grabbed a cold, slippery arm and pulled him onto the flagstones.

He was ugly. Water poured out of his mouth and nose. He was wearing yellow-and-white-striped swim trunks. He had an old scar on his gut, big enough to reach your hand through if you unzipped it. The water dipping off his body spread across the concrete, but nothing else moved. That made me want to kick him in the stomach, hit his face, shake his shoulders until his head rattled, maybe knock him back into the living. It made me want to cry. I didn't hit him, but I stood a long time fighting it down. "You old fool," I said to his dead face.

He didn't look apologetic or angry, just wet and dead.

I walked back into the kitchen with my Glock in my hand and my finger on the trigger. Three days earlier, the judge had said he swam every day when he got up. If he climbed into the pool at dawn, that meant he'd gotten shot in the last half hour. Whoever had shot him might still be hiding in the house.

And I knew who must have done it. I'd sent the Le brothers running to the judge in search of Bob. They must have staked out the house all night and confronted the judge in the morning. When the judge told them Bob wasn't in the house, Chinh or Lanh had shot him. I was betting on Chinh. I had only one question. Had the judge gotten my warning? If he'd listened to my telephone message and decided to stay in his house anyway, then we shared the blame, and after a month or two, or maybe a couple years, I could forgive myself. If he hadn't listened to the message, then my name was on the bullet that killed him, right alongside Chinh's and Lanh's.

I went upstairs. The judge's master suite faced the patio and, beyond it, the lake. A guest room and another big bedroom he'd converted into an office faced the road. In his bedroom, heavy curtains blocked most of the sunlight. I knew if I opened them, I would see the judge's body lying by the pool, so I left them shut and turned on a bedside lamp. The room had high gray walls, three ceiling fans, and a white rug that looked like no one ever had walked on it. The bed was unmade, and a pair of shorts and a shirt were balled up on the floor. The room opened into a large master bath with a Jacuzzi tub and a shower with the knobs on the outside so you could stay dry while adjusting the temperature. Next to the bathroom, double doors opened out from a big walk-in closet. The shelves were stacked as full and neatly as in a department store. A Browning bolt-action shotgun hung in a nylon bag next to some dress shirts. Too bad the judge hadn't gone swimming with it.

In his office, the light on the answering machine was flashing. I swallowed hard and punched the button. The machine announced, "You have one new message." I closed my eyes and hoped it wasn't from me. A town engineer from Berwyn spoke on the recording; he was calling at the last minute to reschedule the judge's grass-cutting service. Sorry for the inconvenience, he said, and he left a phone number.

I sighed. I chose to believe the judge had gotten my call and deleted the message.

Financial records in the desk and file cabinets showed that the judge controlled BlackLite Productions. It was a small operation, a mom-and-pop business, if mom and pop liked to shoot sex videos. The company distributed the majority of the DVDs in Chicago and Milwaukee, a smaller number in Detroit. A spreadsheet said the company had brought in $212,000 in the last year and spent a little over $203,000 on production. The Judge had nine thousand dollars and a couple dozen finished porn videos to show for his effort.

A drawer of files on the video actresses and actors duplicated the files I'd seen at the BlackLite Productions office, except these also cross-referenced the screen names with real names. I thumbed through them until I found a file for Jade. It named Jade as Hannah Le, and it showed that BlackLite had kept her busy in the months since she started dating Bob. Along with *Facets of Jade,* she'd starred in *Jewel of the Orient, Jade and Her Friends,* and *A Close Shave.* For each of the tapes, the judge had paid her just $3,500. I thumbed through the files for the actors but couldn't find one for Bob. The financial records didn't show the company paying him, either.

I was looking through the last desk drawer when I heard the front door open. Then footsteps came up the stairs—light footsteps. They had to be Chinh's. I moved quickly and silently, hugging the wall next to the door with my back, my Glock in both hands up against my chest, like I was praying, and I suppose I was. The footsteps came to the top of the stairs and passed me in the hall, headed toward the judge's bedroom. I spun slowly, silently out the door and into the hall.

A woman in shorts, running shoes, and a sweatshirt was peering into the bedroom. She heard me, turned and saw me, screamed. It was Carla Pakorian.

"It's all right," I said. She backed into the judge's room, and I followed, keeping an even distance between us. "What are you doing here?" I asked.

She kept her eyes on my gun. "Where's Peter?"

"Tell me why you're—"

"Where's Peter?" she asked again, more frantic.

We weren't getting anywhere with my gun pointing at her, so I lowered it. "Why are you here?"

"I tried calling, but Peter didn't answer. I was worried. Peter's getting old and something could happen to—"

"Something did happen to him," I said, but before I could tell her, she backed to the bed and sat down, as if the tone of my voice let her know what I had to say. I said it anyway. "The judge is dead."

She looked at my gun, afraid again. "Did you kill him?"

"No," I said. "He's by the pool. Shot in the head."

She went to the window and opened the curtain. When she saw the judge lying on the patio, she sank to the floor, her palms pulling against the window glass. I put my gun away and went to her, led her out of the bedroom and away from the window. I helped her downstairs and then called 911. While I was giving the dispatcher the information she needed, Carla walked out onto the patio. I watched through the window as she sat cross-legged in the puddle of water surrounding the judge's body and ran her fingers through his hair. She looked like she was mothering him, soothing a child lying in bed with a fever.

I walked out on the patio and stood beside her. After awhile, she looked up at me with tears in her eyes.

"I'm sorry," I mumbled.

She looked at me as if I had answers that I'll never have. "How could anyone do this? Everyone loved him."

"Yeah," I agreed, "everyone loved him." He'd taught me how to fish. He'd slept in the hospital waiting room while Dad had tests to determine if he'd had a heart attack. He'd once been like a second father to me. What wasn't to love? I thought about Chinh and Lanh. They didn't even know the judge well enough to love him or to hate him. "I'm pretty sure the guys who did this were gunning for Bob, not the judge," I said.

A few minutes later, all the Beverly Shores cops on duty roared up to the judge's house. It seemed the cops in Beverly Shores knew and loved the judge, too.

The lead detective was a woman named Lori Rolison, and it turned out she and Carla had gone to high school together and still had lunch together once a month. They hugged each other, and Carla sobbed. Small-town murders: Everyone knows everyone.

The cops yellow-taped the front door and dusted for prints. They walked the patio, looking for a bullet casing or any other scrap the killer might have dropped. They circled the lawn around the patio and picked through the leaves and branches of the azaleas that bordered the backyard fence, as if they were looking for aphids. They crossed into the neighbors' yards and searched the bushes there, too. They secured everything at the scene that I hadn't already tampered with. Rolison charged over to me when another cop told her I'd moved the judge out of the water. "Did you really move the body?"

"I did."

"Didn't you realize you might be destroying evidence?"

"I realized the judge was lying in the water. I wasn't positive he was dead."

She gave me a pained \smile, but then the anger slipped from her face. The damage, whatever it was, had been done. I liked her; she was smart and knew getting angry with me was a waste of energy. "Okay," she said. "I'll want a description of where you found the body, body position, anything else you can think of."

"Done," I said.

Almost as an afterthought, she asked, "You touch anything else?"

"Yeah, I searched the office upstairs."

She lowered her eyelids. "Why did you do that?"

"Curious what I would find."

She shook her head, disgusted. "And what *did* you find?"

"Mostly stuff to do with the judge's hobby."

"Fishing?"

"Photography."

"I didn't know he did photography."

"Even our best friends don't know our secrets."

She tightened her lips. "Keep your hands off from now on, all right?" She turned away.

"I looked through the bedroom, too."

She ignored that. I was a fly in the investigation.

"You want to know who shot him?"

She turned back slowly. "You find that information in the bedroom?"

"I didn't find it anywhere. You want to be looking for two guys named Chinh and Lanh Le."

"Couldn't be," she said.

Her confidence surprised me. "Why not?"

"We've had them in lockup since a little after one A.M. We caught them breaking into the judge's house. The judge was alive then."

"Really?"

"Yes, really." She turned away again. She even waved her hand at me, like she was trying to shoo me away. She walked over to watch the forensics guy take a rough measurement of the hole in the judge's cranium.

Meantime, Carla was weeping on the living room couch. Someone had brought her a blanket and she wore it over her shoulders. She looked like they'd pulled *her* from the pool. Two uniformed cops took her story in writing, and after they were done Detective Rolison walked over and sat with her. Rolison hugged her again.

I sat down on Carla's other side, and Rolison gave me a mean glance, but she didn't tell me to go away. She asked Carla, "Were you with Peter last night?"

She shook her head. "He went out drinking with a man named Ben Turner."

For a guy hired to clear Bob, Turner spent a lot of time drinking with the judge.

"That was early in the evening," Rolison said. "How about later? Did he go over to your house?"

"No."

"At about twelve-thirty, he reported a break-in," Rolison said. "The officers who responded made two arrests, but they told him he should spend the night somewhere else. He said he would stay with a friend. I thought that friend might be you."

Tears formed in Carla's eyes again. "I wish it had been."

"His bed is unmade. He could have ignored the officers' advice," I said.

Rolison narrowed her eyes at me. She said to Carla, "We're pretty sure he didn't spend the night here. Do you know what friend he meant?"

The tears rolled down Carla's cheeks now and she shook her head.

"Okay," Rolison said. "Why don't you go home. Do you think you can drive?"

"Yes," she said.

But Rolison looked her over again and decided otherwise. "I think someone should give you a ride. Can you handle that, Mr. Kozmarski?"

Her question stung like a fly swatter. "Yes, ma'am," I said.

TWENTY

CARLA CRIED IN THE front seat as I drove her home. If my guess was right about the bruises I'd seen on her arms, the judge had hurt her, but still she cried for him. Why did she care about the judge? Why did I? Maybe you allow only someone you love to hurt you that way, I thought.

Learning about the judge's porn sideline would hurt if she didn't already know about it, so, without naming specifics, I asked, "What can you tell me about the judge's video company?"

"BlackLite? What do you want to know?"

So much for hurting her. "Why did he run the company like it was such a secret?"

"Everyone close to him knew he did it. I didn't like it, but it was fun and games for him and his friends. Another way to enjoy his money."

"He kept the company pretty well hidden from the

public, though. Stores paid cash up front for the merchandise. He didn't pay taxes. He didn't advertise."

"Getting kicked off the bench hurt him. I don't think he ever got over it. I know he didn't have much of a public reputation anymore, but he wanted to protect what remained."

"He started a porn company to protect his reputation?"

"He kept it underground. Besides, if people had found out about the videos, he probably wouldn't have gotten a lot of new municipal contracts."

"You're an attractive woman. What did you see in him?"

"Peter was a broken man. Lonely. He needed me."

"And that was enough for you?"

"What could be more than that?"

Five A-frame condos appeared on the roadside, each painted a different bright color. Hers was the green one in the middle. We pulled into a parking space in front of it, then sat quiet for a while. She seemed to be working up the nerve to say something.

"I'm going to ask you something that's hard for me to ask." She hesitated. "But it would help me—it would help right now—not to think about this. Do you know what I mean?"

"No." I shook my head. "I've got no idea."

"Do you want me to—Could I—" She stopped talking and shook her head as if disgusted with herself. Then she put her hand high on my thigh and left it there. I said nothing. Her hand moved to my zipper.

I understood now. When things were bad, I'd sometimes used sex the same way, to forget for a while: ten minutes, twenty, maybe an hour or two, for a whole year and a half with Corrine, until sex got wrapped up in everything else. Maybe Carla sensed that I understood and that's why she chose me to help her forget.

She kissed me on the mouth and neck. The kisses came hard, then soft and desperate, as though she would die if I tried to stop them.

"Let's go inside," I said.

"Yes."

An old yardman cutting the grass in front of her condo eyed us nervously as we walked to the house.

Inside was airy and bright. An enormous window faced out the back of the house over gently sloping sand dunes. The living room had a big round white rug on the hardwood floor, a black sofa with pink throw pillows, a black ottoman, and two pink upholstered chairs.

"I need a drink," she said. "You want one?"

I'd told myself I would never drink again. Besides, it was 8:30 in the morning, much too early to start drinking. "Bourbon, no ice," I said.

She poured me three fingers of Maker's Mark, then four fingers of Beefeater gin for herself. "Cheers."

"Cheers."

We drank, and then she lifted her sweatshirt over her head and unfastened her bra.

"Make love to me," she said.

I shook my head. "Let me hold you for a while."

"I need you to—" I took her hand and led her to her

bedroom. We lay together, with her in my arms, and she said, "I want you to—" But I didn't, and she sobbed in my arms, and after a while she fell asleep. And when she awoke, she said, "Thank you," as if I had.

Then we lay side by side for a long time, trying to hold off the world of pain outside. She broke first. "Do you think Peter was wrong to make the videos?"

I shook my head. "With sex, a lot of the time I don't know what's right and wrong."

"But you thought it would be wrong with me."

"I wanted to, but I'm with someone else."

"Married?"

"It's more complicated than that."

She managed a little smile. "If you had Peter's money, would you spend it like he did?"

I thought of Florida and the best fishing boat money could buy. "If I had money like that, I don't know what I would do."

"If you could buy whatever you desired, whatever made you feel good, you wouldn't do it?"

"What I want isn't always what makes me feel good, so it gets tricky."

"Yeah, me too," she said.

I touched the bruises on her arms. "Did the judge do this to you?"

"Peter? Oh, God no."

"Then who?"

She rolled on her back, then turned to me again. "Bob."

It shouldn't have surprised me. "What happened?"

She hesitated again, then decided to trust me. "After

you left Peter's house on Tuesday, Bob got mad at him for hiring you. Peter hadn't told him you were coming or that he planned to hire you. He waited until you arrived. Bob said Peter was doing it for personal reasons, not because of him. They argued, and I told Bob that if he treated women better, the police wouldn't think he'd killed Hannah. And I said the rest of us wouldn't think so, either. He grabbed me, hard. I guess I pushed it too far."

"No, *he* pushed too far. Do you think he killed Hannah?"

"I don't know what to think. I guess he was capable of doing something like that. I met Hannah a couple times—she was a wild girl, pretty messed up—and Bob reacts strongly to wild, messed-up girls. I've seen it before."

I told her about the video that showed Bob slashing Hannah's blue robe and about Ahmed Hassan's murder and Bill Gubman's shooting. I described the deliveryman and asked if Bob delivered the videos himself or if she'd ever seen Bob in a yellow hat.

She got out of bed, put on a shirt, and went into the living room. When she came back, she had an envelope of photographs. She leafed through them and handed me one. It showed the judge and Bob standing on the judge's patio, holding cans of beer. The judge had on the same yellow- and white-striped swimsuit I found him in earlier. Bob had on a blue swimsuit and a yellow baseball cap. "Like that?" she asked.

I nodded. "Can I keep the picture for a while?"

"Take it. It's yours."

In the picture, Bob was grinning. I frowned back at him.

"Do you know where Bob is now?" she asked.

I shook my head. "But Ben Turner tucked him away somewhere. So I'll find him."

She kissed me on the lips, then on the forehead. "Be careful."

OUT IN LUCINDA'S CAR, I called Ben Turner's office. It was after ten o'clock. Turner's receptionist put me through to his office, and he picked up the phone. He sounded angry. "Where the hell have you been? I left messages for you."

"I've been working."

"I need everyone in right away. You, too."

"You know, I got so excited by the phone records you gave me, I stopped answering my messages."

"Fuck the phone records. They don't matter."

"Fuck you."

"What?"

"Fuck you."

"Fuck me? Fuck *you*! You're out. I talk to Peter this morning, and you're gone. Easy."

"The judge is dead."

"The judge is—Fuck you! I was with him last night."

"This morning, he's dead. Shot in the forehead. Small-caliber weapon. Floating in his swimming pool."

"Fuck!"

"Where's Bob?"

"Where's— That's why I want you in. Piedras has

gone AWOL. We're looking for him now. The word is the state attorney is charging him with Le Thi Hanh's murder this morning."

"Where was he staying?"

"With the girl's lawyer brother, Tuan Le."

"Hannah's brother? Bob told me he was overseas."

"Wake up, okay? He lied. We didn't want anyone to know where he was."

"Why would Tuan let Bob stay with him?"

"He doesn't think Piedras killed his sister. At least he didn't until the asshole went AWOL."

"You know Hannah's younger brothers are gunning for him. You don't want him on the street."

"Look, I can use all the help I can get right now. I want you at my office *now*, okay?"

"I think you lost control of this one."

"Huh?"

"I think you fucked up bad. It's out of control."

"Fuck you!" he said, and hung up.

TWENTY-ONE

I DIALED 411 AND asked for the number of the American Bar Association, then called it and said I was looking for a Chicago lawyer named Tuan Le. Five minutes later, I was speeding toward the firm Selantis, O'Keefe & Johansson.

As I drove, I called Lucinda at the District Eighteen station.

She answered the phone, "Juarez."

"The judge is dead," I said.

"Did you kill him?"

"Why does everyone keep asking me that?"

"Sorry. What happened?"

I told her, though I left out the part about Carla.

She gave me five seconds of sympathy, then said, "You find out where Piedras is?"

"I found out where he *was*. Turner says he skipped from there. He was staying with Hannah's lawyer brother. I'm heading to talk to him now."

"You don't take Piedras without me, Joe." It was a threat.

"I already promised."

"Okay. I've got the file on the earlier charges against him. I see why the state attorney got a hard on for him. The charges are good enough to hang Hannah's murder on him."

"Yeah?"

"Piedras pulled a knife on the other girlfriend, held it to her throat, and threatened her."

"That does it, doesn't it? Turner says the state attorney will charge him this morning. When did he threaten the girl?"

"About four months ago."

"A couple months after he started seeing Hannah. What happened to the charges?"

"Same thing that always happens. Complainant refused to testify. She got scared. Or she thought if she dropped the charges, he'd reform and they'd be married by next Valentine's Day."

I passed two semis, and the South Side of Chicago came into view. Gray, black, white—all that glass, concrete, and steel.

"What are you going to do now?" I asked.

"I'm going back to BlackLite Productions. Maybe something there will point toward Piedras."

"Did the Franklin Park cops okay another search?"

"Hell no."

"Right. Let me know what you find."

She paused. "One more thing."

"Yeah?"

"Later on, I want to talk about last night."

I knew she meant her hand on my leg. "What about last night?"

"I feel like you led me on."

"I'm pretty confused right now."

"Yeah, that's what I want to talk about."

Like we didn't have enough to worry about already. "Okay," I said. "Later on." I accelerated and slipped out from behind a station wagon, squeezed between a pickup truck and an SUV, and sped into an open lane. "Did you get Jason to school all right?"

"Hey, you remembered the kid."

"Drop it, okay?"

"Yeah, I got him to school. I think he liked finding me there this morning."

"He might have ideas about you and me."

"It's not *his* ideas that worry me," she said.

Twenty minutes later, I parked outside the law offices of Selantis, O'Keefe & Johansson.

The firm's reception area had teak trim and a carpet so thick and soft, it made you want to take off your shoes and skip. A couple receptionists talked into phone headsets in hushed voices. The wheels of law ran oil-quiet if you could afford a legal firm like Selantis, O'Keefe & Johansson.

One of the receptionists took my name and the reason for my visit. "Mr. Le is with a client, but if you'll take a chair, I'll let him know you're waiting." The chairs looked like they'd been upholstered for people who'd never sat down on anything hard in their lives. I paced until I started wearing a path in the rug. When both receptionists got busy with calls, I walked into the office area through two big wooden doors.

The plush carpet continued into the hall and offices, though the firm had cut back on the teak. Little brass plates on the doors named the lawyers who occupied the offices. Tuan Le's office was empty, but in a conference room next door to it, an Asian man sat with an old woman. The man was thin and pretty and looked a lot like the pictures I'd seen of Le Thi Hanh. He and the old woman were finishing their meeting, and he was making little stacks of letter-size paper. He tapped each stack square against the table as neatly and delicately as a florist arranges tulips. The old woman smiled contentedly. She was leaving the world soon. All she owned was in the competent hands of Tuan Le.

I knocked on the door and walked in. "Are we almost finished here, Tuan?"

He smiled. "Yes, we are. Almost finished." Only his eyes showed confusion over who I was. "We need about five more minutes."

I looked at my watch impatiently. "I'm sorry, but we were supposed to start the deposition ten minutes ago." I crossed to the conference table and handed a stack of papers to the woman. "I apologize, ma'am, but we messed up horribly, and now Mr. Burleigh's children are as mad as hornets." I took the old woman's elbow and escorted her toward the door.

"Um, *those* copies are mine," Tuan Le said, and he pointed a thin finger at the papers in the woman's hands. He exchanged stacks with her, then gave her a little bow. "We'll continue this next Friday, Mrs. Boyd," he said, and she scurried out of the room.

Tuan's smile disappeared as soon as she was out the door. "Who the hell are you?"

"The bow must charm the old ladies. Where'd you learn to do it—Harvard Law or Yale?"

He cocked his head and looked at me as if he wasn't sure if I was man, fish, or fowl. "I went to Northwestern. Now, please tell me who you are and what you want."

I gave him one of my cards. "I'm Joe Kozmarski, and I'm investigating your sister's death."

"You're working for Judge Rifkin?"

"Was working. The judge is dead."

Except for a twitch in his cheek, he showed no emotion. "What happened?"

"Bob shot him in the head this morning." It seemed as good a guess as any, and I was curious to see Tuan Le's reaction.

It got another twitch from him. "Have the police arrested him?"

"No one knows where he is. But I hear he was staying with you."

"Until two days ago, he was."

"Could you tell me why you let him stay with you?"

"Because he asked. And because he's a friend. Hanh introduced me to him shortly after she started seeing him. I like him. And I trust him. Aside from me, he showed more concern about her than anyone else."

"How about your brothers?"

"Lanh and Chinh are idiots. They didn't care about her when she was alive, so why should they care now? Bob took good care of her. I think he loved her. He provided her with an apartment. And he was helping her in other ways."

"Like?"

"Hanh had a drug problem. Bob arranged counseling."

"Was it working?"

He gave me a thin-lipped smile. "Not that I know of."

"So you gave him a bedroom to lie low in when the police were after him."

"Judge Rifkin's idea. It seemed like a good one. Who would think he'd hide with the victim's brother?"

"Not me."

"How do you know Bob shot Judge Rifkin?"

"I don't," I admitted. "Just seems he's around a lot when people are getting shot or killed."

"You mean my sister?"

I nodded.

"Bob didn't kill Hanh."

His confidence disgusted me. "You know, four months before your sister was stabbed to death, Bob was arrested for pulling a knife on another girlfriend."

He blinked. "The other girlfriend was a nutcase. The charges were dropped. Bob didn't kill my sister."

"How do you know?"

"He was with me the night she died."

"You're kidding."

He shrugged. "I was at Club Nine when Hanh left. He was angry and wanted to go after her, but I calmed him down and talked him into going back to my apartment for a drink. We opened a bottle of scotch and got drunk. He passed out on my couch and didn't leave until the next morning."

"Bob didn't mention spending the night at your apartment."

"Ask *him* why. Don't ask me."

"Did you tell the police?"

"Bob told me not to."

"I suppose no one saw you together. A cabdriver or a doorman?"

"I drove my own car to Club Nine. No doorman. I live alone."

"Not a very airtight story."

He showed me his palms, as if resting his case.

"What's the name of the counselor Hanh was seeing?"

"Why do you want to know?"

"I used to have a bad bourbon habit. I'm thinking of starting up again."

With the smallest hint of a smile, he said, "You seem like a fool, Mr. Kozmarski. Are you one? The man is a psychiatrist who also does psychological therapy. He's not a counselor. His name is Holcombe. Patrick Holcombe." He picked up the remaining stacks of paper from the conference table.

"Do you know where Bob is now?" I asked.

The twitch. "No."

"Would you tell me if you did?"

A little more of a smile. "Probably not."

"Attorney-client privilege?"

He shook his head. "I'm not Bob's attorney. I'm his friend."

"You seem more concerned about Bob than about your sister."

He turned to me again, looked me hard in the eyes. "My sister is dead, Mr. Kozmarski. Bob is living."

"Yeah, I guess that's my point."

He raised his upper lip. I was finally annoying him. "I'm an estate lawyer. On an average, one of my clients dies every two weeks. Do you know what I do when they die? I send a condolence card to the family. I attend the funeral if it's a long-term client. And then I go home, pour myself a scotch, and say, 'Who the hell cares?' I don't. They don't. They're dead. Care about them when they're living. Screw them when they're dead."

"We're not talking about a client. We're talking about your sister."

"What's the difference? She's dead."

"Did you know about the videos Bob was making with her?"

The twitch. "What videos?"

"I'll send you copies."

He was cold, but the twitch said something deep in him was hurting.

TWENTY-TWO

PATRICK HOLCOMBE'S OFFICE WAS on the first floor of a five-story gray-stone building on Oak Street. Double glass doors opened from the outside into the waiting room. Double doors: you could escape through them if you wanted to, but who would want to with a waiting room like this? An overstuffed sofa stood at one end, a painted screen of birds fluttering above cherry blossoms behind it. An overstuffed chair with an ottoman stood in another corner. There was a coffee table with magazines and a wicker table with a vase of dried ferns and pussy willows. Soft music piped in from speakers in the ceiling.

The place was too soothing. It made me tense, itchy.

I knocked on the glass partition that separated the waiting room from the receptionist, and a pale, vacant-eyed woman slid the window open. She bid me good afternoon, and I gave her my card and told her I wanted to talk to Dr. Holcombe and that I didn't have an appointment.

She looked worried, but told me to wait. The window slid closed, and she disappeared.

Ten minutes passed. I knocked on the partition again. Nothing. I tried to slide the window open. Latched from the inside. Five more minutes. The doctor and his receptionist could have slipped out the back and gone to lunch; they could be ripping up my business card and interpreting the pieces like Rorschach blots.

A skinny woman in tight black pants and a tight sweater came in with a slovenly boy around fourteen years old. He was punching buttons on a Game Boy and looked angrier than a cornered cat. He flopped onto the sofa and kicked his sneakers up on the pillows. That could be Jason in three years if someone didn't take care of him, I thought. The woman shouldered past me and knocked on the glass partition. No one answered, so she sat down in an overstuffed chair. She hissed at the boy to take his feet off the cushions, but he ignored her.

Then the door leading to the office area opened about eight inches and a man's head poked out. He had round, gold-rimmed glasses, short gray hair, and a short gray beard. He peered slowly around the room as if he'd lost his keys. "Hello, Steven," he said to the boy. "I'll be with you in a few minutes." His voice was calm, slow, warm. The kid punched at the Game Boy, said nothing. The man nodded toward me and asked, "Mr. Kozmarski?"

I followed him back into a hallway. He had on loafers, khakis, and a maroon vest over a collarless white cotton shirt. "Now," the calm voice said, "I'm Dr. Holcombe. What can I do to help you?"

"I'm investigating Le Thi Hanh's murder," I said.

He grimaced, but then guided me into an office that looked like a smaller version of the waiting room, except it had a set of bookshelves, photographs that were probably of his family, and an old empty cigar display board. He didn't offer me a chair. "You've arrived at my office and interrupted me in the middle of the day without first calling," he said, "and now you're going to ask to see Hannah's file. Am I right?"

"I thought psychiatrists listened first, then talked."

"They listen to their patients. But you're not a patient." He made a show of looking at his watch. "Though I've got one waiting to see me."

"If it would help, I can pretend I think I'm Liz Taylor."

"It would help if you stopped wasting my time and told me what I can do for you."

"I would like to see Hannah's file."

He gave me a tight-lipped smile. "You know I can't show it to you. Everything a patient tells me is confidential."

"Even if she's dead?"

"Dead, incarcerated, out of the country—it doesn't matter."

"Even if what she told you could help catch her killer?"

"What did she say to me that could help catch her killer?"

"She told you about Bob Piedras and about her other lovers: Charlie Morell and the couples she seduced. She told you about the sex videos she made. She told you she liked knives and she liked getting cut as long as the cut wasn't too deep, so you really weren't surprised when you heard she got stabbed to death."

None of that seemed to surprise him. "I was treating her for a drug and alcohol dependency."

"You're talking to an ex-drunk and ex-user, so you're not fooling me. Dependency is wrapped up with everything else."

"So what do you want me to tell you?"

"I figure she also told you she liked it when people watched her, so I want the names of anyone who might have seen the murder being committed. And she probably told you where she went to do the things she did. Did she go first-class all the time, or did she like to slum? I want to check out those places."

He shook his head. "I'm sorry. Without a subpoena, I can't and won't allow—"

"Bob Piedras referred Hannah to you, didn't he?"

He nodded just enough to say yes.

"Why are you protecting him?"

"Protecting—?"

"Is he a patient or a friend?"

"I know him slightly."

"Just slightly? Then why are you protecting him?"

He shook his head like I was crazy. Maybe I was. "I would like you to leave now," he said.

Maybe if I took a lesson from Ben Turner's detectives and punched him in the face a few times, he would give me Hannah's file. But he looked thin-boned, and I didn't want to break his jaw and wreck that calm voice. "You know," I said, "I always figured guys like you wanted to get at the truth, but it seems to me you just want to hide it."

"Get out of my office." He said it calmly.

TWENTY-THREE

MY VISIT TO HOLCOMBE had been a waste of time. I still had the same questions I had when I walked into his office. Why did Tuan Le tell me Bob had spent the night of Hannah's murder at his apartment when no one else had said so, not even Bob, even though the story could set him free? What secrets did Holcombe's calm voice cover up?

I drove out on Clark Street. Unless I'd figured Bob wrong, Tuan Le, like his brothers, should have been gunning for him, but instead he'd treated Bob as if he'd rescued his sister from a riptide. I doglegged onto Lincoln Avenue. The street was lined with high-priced row houses, condos, and town houses. The windows were polished, the brick clean, the paint fresh. A man pushed a stroller down the sidewalk.

What if Tuan Le was telling the truth? What if Bob had saved Hannah from drowning more than once before she went down for good? That wouldn't explain why the bartender had said Bob left the club alone or why Bob didn't tell me he was with Hannah's brother.

I drove across Fullerton, past the DePaul student hangouts, veered onto Sheffield, and drove for a mile past houses that backed up to the El tracks. The houses shook with a death rattle each time a train passed, but they'd stood for a hundred years, some of them, and didn't look like they would fall anytime soon.

A block past Belmont, I pulled to the curb outside Club 9. The marquee advertised "Extreme Dance Friday." The building was dark. I got out and tried the doors anyway. Locked. I shook the doors and knocked on the glass. The bartender probably wouldn't show up until 7:00 or 8:00 P.M. on a Friday.

I called Lucinda to see what she was finding at Black-Lite. Her cell phone rang four times, and her voice mail came on. "Where are you?" I said to the machine. "Give me a call when you can." I called her desk at the District Eighteen station. Another four rings, and my call bounced to an operator. Detective Juarez wasn't in the station. Where else would she be? She always kept a phone nearby. She'd told me once, after she had a couple drinks, that it was the kind of thing lonely people do. I called her home number. Two rings, then the answering machine. I hung up. There was no reason to worry, but I worried anyway.

BlackLite was about an hour away, forty-five minutes if traffic was light and you pushed hard. The afternoon rush hour had started to clog the side streets and expressways. I got there in just under forty minutes.

A gray Chevrolet Impala was parked by the door: an

unmarked Chicago police car, probably the car Lucinda was driving, since she'd loaned me her Civic. Behind the Impala was a red Dodge sedan. Chinh and Lanh. They were out of jail. I unholstered my Glock, took the wooden steps two at a time, and opened the door slowly, quietly.

Lucinda was lying on the floor, her hands above her head, cuffed around a desk leg. She had no shirt on, no bra. Her breasts looked soft and powdered in the fluorescent light, except each of them had a dark red X scratched into the skin. A single drop of blood had rolled down from the cut on her left breast and over her ribs. Chinh straddled her, knife in his hand. He held the knife between her breasts, as if getting ready to make a third mark. Lanh stood behind a camera tripod, recording his brother's game of tic-tac-toe. "Piedras can't be worth this," Chinh said, and he teased Lucinda's skin with the blade. She flattened her body against the floor, but there was nowhere to go.

In three steps, I had the Glock pressed against Chinh's skull. "Put the knife down."

He froze. Lucinda's service pistol was on the desk. He looked at it. Lanh looked at it. If they considered going for it, they must've figured my trigger finger was quicker than their legs. Lanh put his eye back to the camera and kept the video rolling. Chinh stayed frozen and said, "If I push the blade two inches, she's dead." He said it like he was testing out the idea.

"If you break her skin, I'll blow your head off."

He thought about that awhile, then raised the knife and tossed it on the floor.

I picked up Lucinda's pistol and the knife. "Turn off the camera," I said to Lanh. He shrugged and did what I said. I made him and Chinh stand by the wall, hands up where I could see them. Then I lifted the desk leg, and Lucinda pulled the handcuff chain from under it. When she stood, she clenched her hands together and swung at Chinh. She caught him under the jaw and he lifted into the air and fell against the wall. He crumpled as though she'd taken the bones out of his legs. But she went after him anyway. She kicked him in the ribs and stomach; she brought her cuffed hands down on his head again.

She was panting when she finished.

She looked around like a wild-eyed animal. "Where's the handcuff key?"

I didn't see it. Lanh didn't say anything. Chinh couldn't. She spotted it on the floor by the tripod. I picked it up and unlocked the cuffs. She threw them on the floor. She put on her bra and shirt, buttoning the shirt up to her chin, tucking it in deep and tight. She picked up the video camera by the tripod and smashed it on the desk. Plastic, metal, and glass skittered across the room. She found the video chip and stomped on it. Then she picked up the pieces of the chip and looked around the room wildly again. Her eyes stopped on Lanh. "You're going to eat this!" She started toward him.

"Lucinda," I said.

She looked at me, her eyes crazed; then something like sanity returned and she stopped. "Yeah, you're right." But Lanh smirked, and Lucinda spun on him. "You son of a bitch!" I stepped between her and Lanh, and she said, "Get the hell out of my way."

I did.

"Give me my gun," she said.

"No, Lucinda—"

"Give me my fucking gun!"

I held it out to her.

She grabbed it and approached Lanh. "Open your mouth." He smirked. "Open your mouth!" she yelled.

He shook his head.

She swung the pistol up and pressed the barrel against his lips. "Open your mouth."

He opened his mouth.

She smiled and looked at his tonsils. But she didn't shoot him in the teeth, and she didn't stuff the video chip into his throat. She kneed him in the balls.

The big man stood for a moment like nothing had hit him. Then his mouth closed and his jaw clenched; he bent over and fell to the floor. Lucinda stuck the pieces of the chip into her pocket. "This is too good for you," she said.

She sat down on the desk chair, spent. Tears formed in her eyes. "Jesus!" she said. "I don't even know who these guys are."

"Le Thi Hanh's brothers. Chinh and Lanh," I said.

They both started to stir. Lucinda watched them from the desk chair as if she wanted to kill them, but she didn't go after them again. Lanh pulled himself into a crouch, slowly stood up. Chinh took a while longer, and he didn't get past sitting against the wall. He looked at Lucinda like he'd underestimated her.

I sat on the edge of the desk and considered them. "What are we going to do with you boys? Even if the

Beverly Shores cops move fast when they arrest thugs like you and even if your friend Jake Sanders had cash to post bail stuffed in his couch cushions just waiting to be wasted on you, it can't be more than two or three hours since you get out of jail. And already you've assaulted a police officer, a cop in the line of duty. Do you know what happens to guys who assault cops? Every con in the cafeteria line gets a piece of you. There won't be anything left of you by dinnertime."

Lanh didn't look worried. Chinh looked like he wanted to grind me into the floor with a boot.

"It's time to tell us what you know," I said.

"We just want the videos of Hanh," Lanh said.

Chinh said, "And we want Piedras."

"Is that why you shot Ahmed Hassan?"

Lanh said, "Who?"

"The fat guy who ran Stoyz. Bob was delivering DVDs and you ambushed him and Hassan. You probably were gunning for Bob, but Bob surprised you by returning fire, and you hit Hassan."

Lanh said, "We didn't kill anyone, and we never heard of Ahmed Hassan."

Chinh added, "You don't know what you're talking about."

"Yeah, you've told me that before. Okay, I'm stupid. Tell me what I don't know."

"Where's Piedras?" he said.

Lucinda sighed. "Not again."

"Look," I said, "when you've got the knife, you ask us questions. But we've got the knife, and two guns. It's our turn."

Lanh smiled. "And if we don't answer, do you cut us?"

I shook my head. "We shoot you."

"So shoot us," he said.

Lucinda and I glanced at each other. We shrugged. She pointed her pistol at Chinh, put her finger on the trigger. I pointed my gun at Lanh, did the same.

Chinh pressed himself into the wall. Lanh still didn't look worried. We stayed like that awhile.

Then I said, "Bob was staying with your brother Tuan."

Lanh's eyes flashed with anger, but he nodded like he knew it must be true. "'*Was* staying'?"

"He skipped out a couple of days ago. Tuan says he doesn't know where Piedras is. That might be true, might not be. If you threaten to cut him, he might tell you more than he told me."

Lanh looked at me straight. "You really don't know where to find Piedras?"

"No."

He glanced at Lucinda. "You?"

"No," she said.

He nodded again. "Then we're done here." He offered a hand to Chinh.

"Uh-uh," I said, and I hopped off the desk, moved in close to him, gun aimed at his chest. "Now you talk. Why did you come here?"

Lanh frowned and lowered his eyelids halfway; he was just barely tolerating me. "Same reason you and the lady cop did. To see if we could find Piedras or figure out where he's hiding. Also to see if there were any more videos."

"What did you find?"

He waved a finger at Lucinda. "Lady cop did the work for us."

Lucinda let the "lady cop" slide. "I didn't find anything on Piedras," she said. "But I found receipts showing where they warehouse the videos."

"Don't be surprised if you hear about a fire on the southwest side tonight," Lanh said.

I shook my head. "You've got to have very long arms if you can light a match from a jail cell."

"We're not going to jail."

I grinned at him. "No? How do you figure that?"

He said, "I figure you're pretending to be more than you really are. So Chinh and I are going to walk out of here, and you won't stop us."

I glanced at Lucinda and grinned at her, too. "You hear that? They aren't going to jail."

I shouldn't have glanced at Lucinda.

Lanh snatched the gun out of my hand and in a moment the barrel was against my throat.

Lucinda still had her gun aimed at Chinh, but if she shot him, Lanh would shoot me. After what Chinh had done to her, it might be a fair trade. But she let Lanh take her gun, too. He also took Chinh's knife from me and handed it to his brother. He helped Chinh to his feet, then took the clip out of my gun and threw the gun at me. I had a spare clip in my pocket, but I left it there. He took the clip out of Lucinda's pistol, too, and handed the gun to her gently. "I'm sorry about this," he said.

"Sorry won't take care of it," she replied.

He turned toward the door.

"You still assaulted a police officer in the line of duty," I said.

He shook his head as if I was boring him. "You're outside city limits. That means no one's on duty. You're not supposed to be here, either, right? Does the lady cop want to report the incident and let everyone know where she was when she was supposed to be downtown writing parking tickets?"

"When I kicked you in the balls," Lucinda said, "I'm pretty sure I felt something rupture. I'll feel really bad if you start pissing blood."

Lanh nodded like he half-expected it to happen and didn't fully blame her. "Yeah, me, too." He and Chinh started out the door. "Me, too," he repeated to himself.

We heard their car drive away.

"Fuck them," said Lucinda.

"What else did you find?" I asked.

She smiled and pulled three keys out of her pocket, the kind of keys that motels used before they went electric and magnetic, the kind cheap old motels still sometimes used. They had blue plastic diamond tags with the numbers 7, 9, and 11. The keys didn't name the motel they'd come from, but if we could find the rooms they belonged to, I was willing to bet we would find Bob. I had met a girl who was humping her boyfriend in Charlie Morell's strobe-lit basement and she said Bob liked to screw his new girlfriends in a cheap motel on Superior. The girl's name was Jamie; she hadn't told me her last name. She hadn't told me the name of the motel, either, though I also was willing to bet she remembered it.

I called the School of the Art Institute and asked for Morell's office. His phone rang and then his voice mail came on. I got his home phone number from 411 and tried it next. He picked up the phone and sounded like he was sleeping or high. I told him who I was and asked how I could find Jamie.

He said, "Did you wreck my stereo?"

"Yeah, I pulled the speaker wires out of the back. Where can I find Jamie?"

"Never mess with a man's music." He hung up.

I punched his number into the phone again.

"Let me try," Lucinda said.

When he answered, she said in the sweetest voice a boy could ever hope to hear, "Hi, my name's Lucinda." She walked to the other end of the office and talked in a low, soft voice. After a minute or so of that, she hung up.

"He says to try Club Nine tonight," she said.

"What did you say to him?"

"I told him what I would do with his speaker wires if he didn't tell me where she was."

TWENTY-FOUR

IT WAS ALMOST FIVE o'clock. Club 9 wouldn't open for a few hours, and I had a little boy waiting for me at home. I'd gotten an hour of sleep the previous night. I needed a break.

"Want to have dinner at my house?" I asked Lucinda. She shook her head. "I'm going home to take a bath."

"If you want, you can use the shower at my house."

She followed me back into the city. On the way, I called Carson's and ordered barbecue. Then I called Jason and told him to put three plates on the table. When we hung up, I called Bill's room at the Rush Oak Park Hospital. He answered the phone himself, and his voice sounded strong.

I said, "You're the first good news I've heard all day."

"The doctor thinks I'm going to make it. Only hitch is, I've got to take a vacation for a month or two."

"Vacation's a hitch?"

"Yeah, I'll get restless, drive Eileen crazy."

"She there with you now?"

"Tucked in the covers with me."

"Crazy happy, I figure."

"I don't know. I think Eileen's the only one who's not happy I'm alive." I could picture him grinning. "You know, I woke up this morning, and what's the first thing I see? She's coming on to a male nurse. Next thing, she'll be pulling out my IV while I'm sleeping."

I knew Eileen was smiling when he said it. I knew she had tears of happiness in her eyes. I felt water in mine, too.

"You get the guy who put lead in me?" he asked.

"I'm working on it."

"You're a good man, Joe."

"We don't have him yet. Lucinda and I are going after him tonight. He looks good for your shooting, Ahmed Hassan's death, and another killing or two."

"Be careful," he said. "That guy's bullets hurt."

"You can visit him in jail while you're on vacation."

"That's the kind of trip I could relax on."

"Tell Eileen to give you a kiss for me."

"Nah. I'll tell her to give me one for herself."

JASON SET THE DINING room table with candles and place mats, which at my house was the whole works. I hadn't finished putting up the Sheetrock in the dining room, and dust carpeted the floor, but the room felt good with the three of us in it. Lucinda had come out of the shower, hair wet, face scrubbed, looking like she'd spent her life dancing in grassy meadows and swimming in cold-water springs. She scooped coleslaw into a bowl and I slid two slabs of baby-back ribs, half a barbecued chicken, and a bag of french fries onto a tray.

Jason sat between us at the table. "What did you do today?" he asked, as if he was the responsible one at the table.

I thought of the judge's dead body floating in his pool, Carla Pakorian in tears, the two X's carved into Lucinda's breasts. "We made the world safer for boys and girls," I said.

He rolled his eyes and turned to Lucinda. "Is he always like this?"

She nodded. "Even when he's sleeping."

"How do you know what I'm like when I'm sleeping?"

"With some people, you can just tell."

Jason nodded.

"What did you do at school?" Lucinda asked.

He looked at me. "I made two new friends."

Lucinda leaned toward him and raised her eyebrows. "Are they both pretty?"

Jason laughed. "One of them is. But not as pretty as you."

"This kid's going to be dangerous at eighteen," I said.

He grinned. "I'm dangerous at eleven." Then to Lucinda: "Is Joe dangerous?"

She glanced at me. "He's dangerous in many, many ways."

That made Jason happy, and—I don't know why—it made me happy, too. My dining room was where Jason wanted to be right then, and that was good. It also was where I wanted to be.

We ate everything, but Jason was still hungry, so I got up to make him a peanut butter and jelly sandwich. He followed me into the kitchen. "Corrine called a couple times," he whispered, like it was a secret he didn't want Lucinda to hear.

"Did you tell her I would be home for dinner?"

He shrugged, which meant he hadn't told her.

I wondered why she hadn't tried me on my cell phone. Maybe she was calling my house to see if the kid who'd jumped into the middle of our plans to get back together was real or just a bad dream.

Right then, the phone rang. Corrine, I thought, calling to check again.

The voice on the other end was a woman's—sexy and sleepy and drunk. It drew me to it the way the deep open air over a building ledge or a bridge railing pulls and you don't go too close because the tug at the edge might be stronger than you are. "Come see me tonight," Carla Pakorian said. She sounded like she'd worked through the rest of the Beefeater and had sent out for more.

"I would like to," I said, "but I don't think I can. I'm meeting someone tonight who can tell me what I need to finish this thing up. I've got to go back to the judge's club and—"

"What are you doing now?" she asked, as if she wasn't listening.

"I'm eating dinner. How about you?"

"You know," she said.

"No, I don't."

"What are you doing with your hands?"

"I'm making a peanut butter sandwich."

For some reason, she laughed at that. "You want to know what I'm doing with mine?"

"Look, I'm using a knife. Don't make me slip and cut myself."

Carla laughed again, but she told me anyway.

I didn't cut myself, but I'm pretty sure I blushed.

"When you're done at Club Nine, come and wake me, okay?"

"I'll try," I said. "But don't wait up expecting me."

"Bring a bottle of gin. And more bourbon if you want."

"I'll do what I can," I said.

"I'll leave the door unlocked."

She needed company, but, bad as I felt for her, it wasn't going to be me.

We washed the dishes, and then Lucinda and I had coffee while Jason packed a suitcase with clothes for the weekend. Around 8:30, we drove him to Mom's house.

We went inside together and Mom looked glad to meet Lucinda, until Jason gave her and me a kiss and then lugged his suitcase upstairs. "Not even a week together," she said, suspicious, "and already you've got a nice little family. A little too fast and cozy, if you ask me."

"Cut it out, Mom," I said.

She turned to Lucinda and pointed a thumb at me. "You can't turn a cat into a canary. Not unless you want the bird to chew its own head off."

I said, "Can canaries chew?"

She gave me cold eyes. "If they used to be cats, they can."

"Look, you're the one who moved the kid into my house."

"A little too fast and cozy, if you ask me," she repeated.

OUT IN THE CAR, Lucinda looked at me awhile before starting the engine. "Maybe your mom's right," she said. "Maybe this is a bad idea."

"What's a bad idea? Nothing's going on. We're just doing what we're doing, right? I'm not doing anything. Are you?"

"You're not making sense. But no, I'm not doing anything."

"Then let's just do what we're doing, okay?"

"Sure."

She kept her eyes on the road, and neither of us said anything else on the drive to Club 9.

TWENTY-FIVE

A LINE TWENTY DEEP stood at the entrance to the club. The women wore short shorts or miniskirts, the men shirts that showed their muscles. A short beefy guy in black pants, sunglasses, and a white T-shirt three sizes too small stood behind a rope cordon. He checked out each of the club hoppers and let them in through the tinted doors. He checked the IDs of two girls who looked sixteen, but when one of them gave him a hug and ran her fingers through his hair, he let them in, too.

When Lucinda and I got to the front of the line, he crossed his arms over his chest and flexed his muscles. He looked me up and down. My jeans were clean; so were my shirt and gray jacket. But they didn't impress him. Neither did Lucinda's jeans and cotton shirt. "What do you want?" he asked.

"First, I want the secret of those biceps. Are they real or implants? Then I want to run my fingers through your hair like that sixteen-year-old you just let in," I said.

The arms stayed crossed, but he stopped flexing. "Leona's is up the street," he said. "They make a good pizza, and they'd be happy to have you there. They're open till midnight. Why don't you give them a try?"

Lucinda stepped closer and flipped open her badge. "Because we're really itching to dance tonight."

He gave us a welcoming grin. "Why didn't you say you were on the guest list?"

It wasn't even 10:30, but the club was packed. The air was thick with sweat and alcohol and the burned electrical smell that nightclubs seem to get when things heat up with dance and music. The music was techno and way too loud. The floor was a carpet of bodies, arms waving in the air, arms thrashing, bodies bumping up against one another. It looked about as fun as a bag of squirrels. The kids would have wounds from their night out partying. Women dressed in red-and-black panties danced in the little cages at the top of the four chrome fire poles. A guy stuffed into a little black Speedo, abs like speed bumps, danced in the fifth cage. One of the women slid down her pole, danced on the floor beneath it, and melted into the crowd.

I shouted to Lucinda, "If we can make it to the bar without getting cut in pieces, they'll let us live and make us full members of the tribe."

Either she didn't hear me or she didn't get it. "Yeah, sounds good," she shouted.

I took her hand and we moved into the crush of bodies.

Dim lights hung over the bar. Spotlights shined on the dance cages. The rest of the club swam in red strobes, violet, total darkness, then white diamond sparkles spinning over the dancing bodies. Jamie could be anywhere or nowhere, I thought.

A thick, round-faced girl danced toward us and got in our way. She had on a bright red sarong and a black Miracle bra. She made her breasts do some fancy dance steps and she wiggled her fingers, inviting us to dance with her. We couldn't get around her, so I shouted, "Where's Jamie?"

But she just opened her mouth wide and let a pierced tongue loll at the bottom, then danced away from us.

Lucinda shouted, "Let's go get a pizza at Leona's."

We moved deeper into the swarm.

A dark-haired guy put a hand on my shoulder. He gave me a two-finger salute and yelled, "Charlie's basement."

It was Henry, the guy who'd been doing magic tricks with Jamie's panties when I went to Morell's house. He looked glad to see me, though I couldn't figure why. Far as I could tell, I'd pretty much ruined his date the last time I saw him.

He yelled, "Talk?" and I nodded.

He signaled for me to follow, then pushed into the crowd. Lucinda and I trailed after him before the bodies could close together again.

A couple minutes later, we stood in a stairwell that led to the rest rooms. Two women kissed halfway down the stairs, and the music shook the walls.

Henry glanced at Lucinda, then back to me. "Is she cool?"

"Are you cool?" I asked her.

"Sure," she said.

"Sure," I told him.

"Yesterday, after you left," he said, "Charlie started talking weird. He said he wanted to kill you and Bob Piedras. I don't want to tell this to the cops, but—"

I held out a hand to stop him. "You're telling it to the cops." I introduced Lucinda.

"You said she was cool," he muttered, as if I'd betrayed an old trust.

"She's cool for a cop. But you take your chances."

"Look," he said, "Charlie's a friend. I don't want to hurt him. But he's acting crazy."

"Crazy how?"

"Well, he's got a gun."

"Him and seventy million other Americans."

"Yesterday afternoon, he started shooting it in his basement."

"Was he shooting at anyone or anything in particular?"

He eyed Lucinda for a moment but kept talking. "You asked Jamie about the Chinese robe Bob bought for Hannah. Charlie has two robes of his own: a red one and a yellow one. He hung the red one from the basement ceiling and shot it up. It was in shreds when he got done with it."

"Yeah, that's crazy," I said, and I wondered if either Henry or Charlie knew that Bob had slashed the blue robe on-camera.

"Then he wanted Jamie to put it on."

"And?"

He shrugged, unhappy. "She put it on."

"That's bad," I said.

"Then Jamie told me to leave."

"What did you do?"

"Charlie had a gun. I left."

Lucinda said, "You know what kind of gun?" She was looking for a connection to the judge's shooting.

Henry shook his head. "A pistol, that's all. I don't know about guns."

"Big? Little? Anything unusual about it?"

"Big, I guess. It shredded the robe."

That ruled it out as the gun used to shoot the judge.

"Anything else?" I said.

"I haven't seen Jamie since then. Usually, she comes here every night. Last night, she didn't. I tried Charlie's house, but he said she wasn't with him, either."

That could be very bad, bad enough to wreck the lives of her family and friends for a while. I put a reassuring hand on his shoulder. "We'll find her."

Henry nodded, but he didn't look reassured.

I gave him a card and asked him to call me if he saw Jamie.

Lucinda and I pushed back onto the dance floor and headed for the bar. Jamie was our best lead to Bob, and now she was gone. Morell had told Lucinda we could find her here, but his word was worth nothing. Why had he dressed her up in a shredded robe, a robe that looked like the one Hannah wore before she died? What was his connection to Hannah's death and to Bob? Maybe the bartender I'd talked to earlier in the week could answer our questions. And maybe he could levitate while pouring a vodka tonic. It seemed about as likely.

"Hey, Proud Possum!" he shouted when he saw me across the bar.

"Hey," I said, "we're looking for Jamie."

"Haven't seen her. Not in the last couple nights. You want a drink?" He stepped away without waiting for an answer and filled two glasses with Coke. He brought them back to us, handed one to Lucinda with a smile that probably worked well with women who liked men with big bare-breasted motorcycle chicks tattooed on their biceps. "You're on duty, right?" he said to her.

"Good guess," she replied.

"I don't guess." He tapped his forehead with his index finger. "I know." He handed me my Coke. "And I know you're looking for Bob."

"How do you know that?"

He shrugged. "People talk."

"Yeah, sometimes too much," I said. "But not you. Why didn't you tell me he left with Tuan Le on the night Hannah got killed?"

"He told me not to."

"Why would he do that?"

"Now, that I don't know. You'll need to ask him." He pointed across the dance floor, nodding toward the entrance. Bob was dancing with Jamie. I felt like ordering a vodka tonic and asking the bartender to levitate. Instead, I tipped him ten bucks for the Cokes, and Lucinda and I tried to run across the floor.

We made it about halfway before Bob saw us coming. He gave me a smile that said he recognized me; then he grabbed Jamie's hand and headed for the door. They were outside two or three minutes before we exited the Club.

Lucinda ran north on Sheffield; I ran south.

A block and a half away, I hit Belmont. To the left, the street crowd was partying, just as they did every Friday night. A group of kids were hanging out in front of a vintage clothing store called Pin. The boys and a couple of girls were doing tricks on skateboards. Other girls, in leather or schoolgirl skirts, their bodies pierced from eyebrow to belly, sat smoking on the hoods of cars. A station wagon full of yelling teenagers drove by.

Hundreds of people, but none of them was Bob.

I looked around, helpless. A pair of transvestites passed on the sidewalk, holding hands. One was white with long blond hair, the other black with short hennaed hair. They both had miniskirts and great legs. The black one winked at me.

That was something, but it wasn't Bob. I walked back toward Sheffield. The crowd thinned near the Belmont El station. A few partyers and a couple stragglers stood on the sidewalk. A bike messenger in a black-and-orange nylon bike jersey rode toward me on the street. A drunk in a doorway mumbled when I passed. A south-bound train screeched into the Belmont station. The bike messenger let his wheels glide and looked at me, head cocked to the side, as if he were a poodle and I had made a strange sound. Why was a bike messenger riding on Belmont at 11:00 P.M. on a Friday? I moved forward and the messenger veered off the street and up onto the sidewalk twenty feet from me. He reached into his jersey, and I thought, *I know you.* He was a good-looking black man with a tight Afro. I'd last seen him carrying a six-pack of beer into the kitchen of an over-heated housewife in a video called *Passion Fruit.* He smiled as if he knew me, too, and didn't like me.

His hand came out of the jersey with a silver pistol. I dived to the sidewalk and saw the flash of the gun, heard the bullet's explosion. I rolled once over the pavement and came up with my Glock in my hand. He was looking at me, his gun hand extended toward me, the impossibly dark and deep hole of the gun barrel looking me in the eye, his finger on the trigger, ready to shoot again.

I shot first.

He took the bullet in his ribs and flew off his bike, landed headfirst on the concrete. His pistol slid out into the traffic.

I ran to him. The drunk in the doorway was watching me. The partyers on the street were backing away, keeping their eyes on me, as if I were a pit bull they fig-ured would lunge at them if they showed fear and ran. I turned the messenger over on the sidewalk. His jaw hung sideways, broken, and his mouth was full of blood and pieces of teeth. His eyes were dead.

I reached into his jersey for an ID.

The drunk in the doorway said, "Go." He nodded down the sidewalk toward Sheffield. A tall, burly, bald man ran toward me with a shotgun in his hands. I scrambled the other way, but another man was coming: a tall, skinny man with a pistol.

"The El," the drunk said.

"Smart drunk," I said.

I ran into the Belmont El station just as the man with the shotgun squeezed off a shot. It shattered a store window. I jumped the turnstile and took the stairs three at a time.

Another shot rang against the metal fare booth.

A train stood on the tracks, doors open, a Brown Line train, heading from Ravenswood downtown, a night train, taking its time. I got on the closest car, hung low to the window, and begged the doors to close. The gunmen came up to the platform and, without exchanging a word, ran to opposite ends of the train. They waited until the doors started to shut and then jumped into the end cars. They would be working their way toward me.

We started moving.

The Wellington stop was a quarter mile to the south, half a minute away. I ran to the front of the car, yanked open the metal door, and stepped from one car to another in the rattling night. The bald man with the shotgun was coming toward me, checking every seat, ignoring the panicked riders. I jammed my Glock into its holster, stuck my foot into the outside door handle, and hoisted myself up on top of the train car. A moment later, the bald man came out and crossed to the next door.

I could have shot him in the back of the head if I had had my gun in my hand. But the shaking train also could have thrown me forty feet down to the alley below the tracks if I had tried.

I rode, stomach to cold metal, palms pressed flat. The

dark night flew by overhead. Under me, sparks shot from the rails and burned out in the blackness. As the train slowed for the Wellington station, I slid off the roof and then climbed into the car, where I sat low on the floor.

The gunmen got off, talked with each other, looked forward and back on the platform. The tall, skinny one stepped to the window next to where I was crouching. I knew if he saw me, he would shoot me point-blank.

The bald man paced up and down the platform, swinging his shotgun. My gun was slippery in my sweating hand.

A bell rang somewhere, then rang again.

The bald man yelled, "Fuck!" He charged toward the car where I was hiding, then stopped.

The doors closed and the train jerked forward. It stopped, then jerked forward again. I stayed low in my seat. Except for the shaking that started in my hands and passed through the rest of my body, I didn't move until we reached Armitage, three stops down the line.

TWENTY-SIX

I HUNG IN THE shadows of an empty storefront.
Cars drove by on Armitage. Pigeons in the concrete
work above made a hollow cooing. When I got back
enough nerve to hold my fingers steady, I called Lucinda. She answered her phone. "Where the hell are
you?"

I told her the short version and said to be careful.
Whoever was trying to shoot me might shoot her, too.

"I'm all right," she said. "I ran a couple blocks north
and didn't see Piedras or Jamie, so I went back to my
car. I've been circling Club Nine, looking for you."
She'd already driven by the Belmont El, and there was
no bike messenger lying in a pool of blood and broken
teeth, no bike, no ambulance, no police. Someone had
scooped the messenger off the street and disappeared
with him. Only a drunk, some teenaged skateboarders,
and a transvestite or two remained to tell what had happened, and who was going to believe them?

She said she would pick me up, so I crouched in the shadows, cradling my Glock and considered why three men had tried to gun me down. The bike messenger's appearance in *Passion Fruit* told me he was connected to Bob. Maybe Bob had his own little Secret Service, and when he saw Lucinda and me at the club, he'd signaled them to search and destroy. But Charlie Morell had sent us to the club, and Henry had said Morell had talked about killing me. Had he set us up? The pigeons answered with hollow coos.

Lucinda's Impala rolled to a stop at the curb. I put my gun away and wandered out casually, like I had no worries in the world.

But then a black SUV gunned its engine from around the corner. A big bald man leaned out the passenger-side window. He had a shotgun in his hands. I ran, and he shot. He pumped to reload as I slid into Lucinda's passenger seat. The shooters must have seen Lucinda circling the Belmont El and guessed that she was looking for me.

"Go!" I yelled.

We whipped out from the curb, with the SUV behind us. The shotgun blasted and the back window shattered.

"Shoot the bastard!" Lucinda yelled.

Out the back window, the SUV's grill closed in on us. Lucinda accelerated and I aimed and shot. A hole appeared in the middle of the SUV's windshield, cracks marbling out to the side. The SUV kept coming.

We flew through a stop sign, cut around slow traffic. Streetlights, store lights, and headlights flashed through the car. The SUV held with us, and the bald man leaned out his window. I aimed at the driver's side. The bald man aimed at me.

Lucinda asked, "Okay, what now?" A block and a half away, a stoplight was turning red. A long line of cars were waiting to cross the intersection. She barked a laugh, said, "Alley!"

It looked more like a concrete footpath between two brick apartment buildings. A Dumpster blocked part of the entrance to it.

"No way!" I yelled.

She veered into the right lane. The SUV followed.

"Too tight!" I yelled, and I aimed again. The bald man popped back out of the window and pointed the shotgun at me. I squeezed off two shots. He squared his sights on me, grinned.

Lucinda hit the brakes hard. The SUV driver hit the brakes, but too late. The bald man stopped grinning as the SUV rushed toward us. Lucinda cut the wheel and threaded us into the alley. The SUV followed—almost. It crashed into the brick corner of the apartment building, metal and brick blasting in the night.

The bald man stumbled out of the vehicle as we rolled over the potholes and garbage in the dark alley. We turned left and headed through another alley to the cross street.

We sat at the alley mouth, catching our breath, watching the traffic pass. If we had tried to talk, we would've made sounds that weren't language anyway, sounds like the low guttural noises wild animals make when they're scared. Then Lucinda laughed, and I laughed, too. We laughed a low guttural laugh that we couldn't stop and didn't try to. If the bald guy and his friend had come through the alley behind us while we were laughing, they could have stood beside our windows and executed us, and we wouldn't have raised our hands to cover our faces, we were laughing so hard.

The laughter faded, and after a while it stopped. We caught our breath. We breathed deeply because we were alive and could breathe any way we wanted to.

Lucinda leaned back in her seat and gripped the steering wheel with both hands. "Where now?"

"Let's go talk to Charlie Morell."

"Okay," she said, still steadying herself.

I gestured at the police radio. "You going to call this in?"

"Ten to one, the SUV's stolen. Hundred to one, these guys don't stick around for the police. My guess is they're already gone."

"Why bother?"

"Why bother."

We cruised up Ashland Avenue about five miles under the speed limit until Ashland merged into Clark Street, and then we inched along with the rest of the slow traffic.

Lucinda suddenly bowed her head and closed her eyes. "Damn," she said.

"What?"

She looked up at the rearview mirror and pointed her thumb over her shoulder.

Three cars back, a green Saturn was weaving from lane to lane, punching through the traffic. When the oncoming lane opened up, the Saturn swung out and then squeezed back in, two cars behind us now. The driver was a bald man. A shotgun barrel stuck half a foot out his window.

"How could—?" I said.

"Car jack?"

"He's alone this time."

"Doesn't make me any happier."

I checked the clip in my Glock as the Saturn cut again into the oncoming traffic and swung back in with one car between us. Two laughing girls were in that car. I pointed my Glock over the backseat and motioned for them to stop. They quit laughing, and the driver hit the brakes, boxing in the Saturn.

"Good thinking," Lucinda said.

The Saturn cut into the right lane, swung around the girls, and sped up behind us.

"Not good enough," I said.

The bald man steered with one hand and fumbled with the shotgun at the window with the other. He couldn't get the angle.

"Kill him this time," Lucinda said.

He wove behind us, and I trained my gun on him. He swung into the right lane again and accelerated beside us. We were so close we could have punched each other out of our windows, but we held our guns and looked each other in the eye; I aimed at his face, but I couldn't tell you what expression he had, though he wasn't three feet away.

"Jesus!" Lucinda shouted. Then the bald man's face and eyes and gun disappeared in an explosion of metal and fiberglass. The Saturn had crashed into the back of a delivery truck that had stopped short. The collision jammed the Saturn's horn, and the mournful sound of it followed us up Clark Street. The crash probably hadn't killed the bald man, but this time he didn't stumble out of the car.

We drove for a while without saying anything before I noticed Lucinda moving her lips as if offering a silent prayer.

"What're you thinking?" I asked.

"I'm reevaluating the decisions I've made in my life."

"Yeah?"

"From now on, I'm going to go to church on Sunday. I'm going to check in with my Mom and Dad twice a day. And I'm going to eat healthy food, sleep eight hours a night, pay my bills on time, and see my dentist twice a year. What are *you* thinking?"

"I'm thinking about what I'll do to Morell if it turns out he sent the shooters."

THE LIGHTS WERE OFF in Morell's yellow two-flat building. We rang the doorbell and knocked on the thick wooden door. No one answered.

"You want to go in anyway?" Lucinda asked.

"Give me a minute and I'll take care of the lock."

But Lucinda tried the knob. The front door swung open. "Looks like we're invited." We drew our guns and stepped inside. Lucinda found a switch and lighted up the front hall. The place smelled like rotten food. "We should have gotten that Leona's pizza," she said.

I called, "Charlie!"

Nothing.

"Professor Morell!"

Lucinda went into the living room, turned on a light. A greasy paper bag rested on the floor next to the couch. An empty Mountain Dew bottle stood on the brushed-steel coffee table. Someone had been eating dinner alone. I continued down the hall, went into the dining room, switched on the light. Two cockroaches scurried away from a half-eaten plate of spaghetti. The noodles were hard, probably out in the open for a day or more. Lucinda walked past in the hall, whispered, "I'm telling you, we should've tried Leona's," and continued to the bedroom. As I stepped out of the dining room, she came back out into the hall. She looked shaken.

"Does Morell have a ponytail?" she asked.

"Yeah, a long, thin, rip-cord thing."

She frowned and tipped her head toward the bedroom. I knew I didn't want to look. Why look when you know what you'll see will just make you sadder? But my feet moved down the hall anyway.

Sometimes death is easy. A guy has a couple drinks, takes a shower, brushes his teeth, and goes to bed. He falls asleep and breathes deep sleep-breaths until he doesn't. His heart stops beating, his brain stops firing signals, and his skin turns cold, all as quiet as flipping a wall switch, all as peaceful as a Christmas card.

Charlie Morell's death wasn't like that. He was lying on his bed, wearing the shredded remains of his red ceremonial robe. His ponytail was wrapped around his neck and he clutched it as if he was trying to choke himself. His jaw was clenched so hard, you'd think his teeth would turn to dust. He'd puked through his nose and mouth. Vomit covered his face, his body, the robe, the bed. His skin was as white as skin ever could be.

Lucinda came in behind me. "Looks like an overdose," she said. "And I'd bet a Leona's pizza it was MDMA."

"Ecstasy."

"Yeah, I've seen it. Their body temperature rises to a hundred and seven or eight. They cramp and puke. They grind their teeth. Then they have a heart attack or a stroke. In the bad ones, the kidneys and other organs get hit first."

We left the bedroom and closed the door behind us, walked down the hall into the kitchen. A white envelope leaned against a glass of water on the kitchen table. The letter said all the things suicide letters say and said them no better than most. He apologized to his mother and father and to someone named Eric. They probably would cry when they read it. But the words left me cold.

He wrote about Hannah and rejoining her in death, as if he could crawl out of whatever coffin they put him in and claw through the soil until he reached her casket, then knock three times on the wood and she would say, "Come in, Charlie. Lie with me, heal my wounds." He blamed Bob for her murder, but he didn't give any evidence, and he didn't explain his own connection to him. He said he planned to take twenty-four tablets of ecstasy, but we'd already guessed about that much.

He finished by saying what they all say: The world

would be better off without him. I wasn't in the mood to argue.

Lucinda and I searched the house. In the basement, two twisted coat hangers were nailed to the ceiling near the strobe light. Morell had hung the robe on them before shooting it. A hammer, a handful of nails, and a stepladder were thrown to the side. The concrete wall beyond the hangers was bullet-pocked. A Colt .45 lay on the floor near the couch. We left it there and went back upstairs.

The kitchen, dining room, and living room turned up nothing, so we had to go back into the bedroom. I searched the closet and dresser, keeping my back to Morell, while Lucinda checked the bathroom shelves and medicine cabinet. The yellow ceremonial robe that Henry had mentioned hung from a closet rack in a dry-cleaning bag. Probably not the best way to keep a thing like that, but Morell was the art historian, not me.

When I came out into the bedroom, Lucinda was standing in the bathroom doorway, looking at a couple of prescription bottles.

She tossed one of the bottles to me. "Poor guy. He was on antidepressants."

I read the label. "Zoloft, one-hundred-milligram tablets." No surprise for a suicide to be clinically depressed. But the prescribing doctor was P. Holcombe. And that was worth thinking about.

TWENTY-SEVEN

IF LUCINDA HAD RADIOED in Morell's suicide, she would have had to stick around and work the scene. So, I called 911 from the kitchen, and then we let ourselves out the front door. A light rain made the night black and shiny as obsidian. The air was turning cold again, cold and full of death.

We cruised downtown on Lake Shore Drive and exited at Oak Street, listening to the windshield wipers through the wash and glare of rain. A group of tourists were hanging out under umbrellas by Water Tower Place, and a few people still walked the sidewalks near Holcombe's office, but the weather had sent the Friday-night crowds into bars or coffee shops or home to whatever was waiting for them there. A sign on the double glass doors said Holcombe's office was protected by a security system. "Can't go in the front," Lucinda said. "Not for a couple of hours at least."

"You want to wait a couple of hours?"

She shook her head no.

"I'll be back." A concrete path cut between the gray-stone building where Holcombe had his office and a newer stucco building next door. A locked iron gate was bolted to the sides of the two buildings, but there was no barbed wire on top, so the gate didn't do its job. The path led past garbage cans and an old rusted window air-conditioning unit into a concrete courtyard that stretched the length of three buildings and could have been part of an alley a long time ago. A burglar gate covered the back door to Holcombe's office building. But a window nearby had no bars, just a sign that said NO DRUGS ON PREMISES—that and three alarm sensors the size of nickels stuck to glass.

I broke a windowpane with a piece of concrete block from the courtyard and reached inside to the lock. When I raised the window, an alarm bell rang and kept ringing.

I dropped from the window into a hall. The receptionist's area was down the hall and to the right, and in it two four-drawer lateral file cabinets stood side by side. A hungry squirrel could break through the locks on them.

Hannah had a thick file, and Charlie Morell had a thin one. Bob didn't have a file. I checked for the judge, just on the off chance. Nothing on him, either.

I took Hannah's and Charlie's records and made a quick tour of the rest of the premises. A closet outside Holcombe's inner office had shelves full of drug samples: Celexa, BuSpar, Lexapro, Paxil, Zoloft, a carton of Xanax.

Next to the closet was the bathroom, which was scrubbed clean. The mirror showed a strung-out, tired face: my skin as pale as Morell's, my eyes watery and red. The alarm bell was making my head shake. If the cops came through the front door, they would think I was one of Holcombe's patients looking for a fix.

I went to the window, dropped the files onto the pavement outside, climbed out after them, and walked to the front of the building. Lucinda had the engine running when I got in beside her. As we pulled from the curb, a squad car came around the corner, lights flashing. Behind us, another squad car came from the other direction.

We drove a couple blocks and parked behind a library. Lucinda started through Morell's file, and I took Hannah's. Like Tuan Le had told me, Bob had referred Hannah to Holcombe. An information sheet she'd filled out as a new patient said so. It also said she was five eight, weighed 110 pounds, and had a tattoo of a wasp on her left shoulder. In a long list of possible conditions and complaints, she'd checked boxes for "Excessive drug or alcohol use," "Drug or alcohol dependency," and "Self-destructive behaviors." She hadn't checked boxes for about thirty other problems. There'd been plenty of years when I would have filled out that list the same.

Holcombe's notes said he'd put Hannah on ReVia after her first visit. I knew ReVia from when I'd stopped drinking. It blocks something in your brain so you don't get pleasure from alcohol or narcotics. It works if you want to kick a habit so much that you're willing to give up the pleasure. A lot of people don't want to kick their habits that much. The notes from Hannah's second visit, four weeks later, said she was one of those people. She admitted she hadn't been taking her prescription but said she'd cut back on the drugs and alcohol anyway. She gave Bob credit for her improved behavior. The sex was great. He was great. She felt less need for anything else. Three cheers for Bob.

A month later, she was drinking and using heavily again. She mentioned motels and hotels—no names— and said she was having sex with other men besides Bob, and he was having sex with other women. Maybe she liked to watch men watching her, but something about it was tearing her up. She got drunk or high most nights, and a lot of days, too.

Next time, she was partying just as much as before, but she'd decided to try intensive psychological counseling. They started at the beginning—her life as a schoolgirl growing up in Little Vietnam, her parents, her brothers—and moved quickly to the present. I skimmed through two pages of notes before I got to Bob. She talked about the silent auction where she first saw him and he bought her the robe. Afterward, they'd left together, and he'd taken her to a cheap motel. That had thrilled her. She'd never felt so alive and sexy as when she was standing in a thirty-buck room modeling an eight-thousand-dollar robe. It had thrilled Bob, too. They'd had sex all night long—on the robe, in the robe, under the robe. And it thrilled me, because she named the motel where it had happened. It was called the Parnassus.

A call to 411 gave me an address in the 2200 block of West Superior.

TWENTY-EIGHT

THE PARNASSUS MOTEL WAS a white cinder-block single-story strip of about twenty rooms set back from the street. The parking lot was empty, but Bob probably would have parked on the street somewhere to avoid calling attention to where he was staying. The motel looked like something built shortly after World War II and last renovated in the sixties or early seventies. It needed tearing down.

A steady rain was falling on the grimy white sign out front. The *n* in Parnassus and the *M* in Motel were made to look like mountains. Someone had put a lot of love into designing that sign. A sign below that one said VACANCY. I figured the judge and Bob rented by the month. When they weren't shooting a video, Bob could take his dates there. And when he didn't have a date, he could hide out from a bench warrant.

Lucinda had found keys numbered 7, 9, and 11 at BlackLite, and all three rooms were dark. We went to the office and rang a doorbell outside. After a while, an old man in pajamas and slippers shuffled out from behind a curtained doorway. He pressed a tired face close to the glass. "You want a room?" he shouted.

What I wanted was to avoid yelling about our visit. I said, "We would like to talk with you."

"Thirty bucks, including tax," he shouted. "Cash only. Put it through the mail slot."

"Can we come in?" I asked.

"No." His fingers clanked the aluminum door on the mail slot to show where he wanted the money.

Lucinda pulled out her badge and held it to the glass.

The old man was unimpressed. "I don't care what you do during daylight," he shouted. "If you want a room with this fellow tonight, it's thirty bucks, including tax."

To quiet him, I slipped a twenty and a ten through the slot. "I've got a friend who recommended this place. A guy named Bob Piedras," I said.

He ignored that and shuffled behind the counter. He returned with a room key with the motel's blue plastic diamond tag. He shoved the key through the slot and shouted, "Room four. Thank you and good night." He shuffled back toward the curtain.

"Sir!" I shouted.

He raised both hands, as if begging me to let him go to sleep. "What do you want?"

"Is Bob Piedras staying in one of your rooms?"

He nodded. "He's the only one in the place. Number eleven." And he shuffled away.

Lucinda and I went back to her car. The rain was

coming down harder now, and gusts of wind swept across the windshield and roof. "You want to go in loud or quiet?" she said.

"Quiet."

"Right." She got a flashlight and metal snips out of the trunk.

We ran through the rain to a breezeway between the office and the motel units, then made our way to number 11. I put my ear to the door; everything was quiet. I checked the clip in my Glock. Lucinda used key number 11, opened the door a crack, and snipped the security chain. She turned on the flashlight and we stepped silently into the room.

The flashlight shined on two lovers lying together naked in bed, curled around each other with the gentleness and delicacy that comes only in sleep. I flipped a light switch, and a bare bulb shined down on Bob and Tuan Le. They stirred but didn't open their eyes until Lucinda kicked the bottom of the mattress and shouted, "Wake up, boys."

Bob startled and sat straight up in bed. He pulled the sheets around him up to his shoulders. Half his face was red from pressing against Tuan's shoulder, the other half pale. Tuan grunted and rolled over, pulled a pillow over his head. Lucinda kicked the bottom of one of his feet and said, "Come on. Get up." He did so slowly, then sat leaning against the headboard and yawned.

"You're under arrest," Lucinda said to Bob.

He blinked and, without dropping the covers, held his hands where we could see them.

Tuan finished his yawn. "Am I under arrest, too?"

Lucinda kept her eyes on Bob, nodded. "Aiding and abetting a fugitive."

Tuan Le shook his head in mock dismay. "Is Bob a fugitive?"

I said, "Aiding and abetting an asshole."

Tuan Le stretched his arms and rolled his neck side to side. "All right, then," he said, and he climbed off the bed and walked casually into the bathroom. We heard him pissing long and hard, flushing, running water in the sink.

"What are you arresting me for?" Bob asked.

Lucinda listed the charges. "The murder of Le Thi Hanh, the murder of Ahmed Hassan, the murder of Judge Peter Rifkin, and"—she gave a satisfied smile—"the attempted murder of Detective Bill Gubman."

He shook his head. "Not me. The only one I shot was the detective, and that was self-defense."

"You're a lousy liar," she said. "You don't shoot a man who identifies himself as a police officer, self-defense or not."

"He didn't identify himself."

Lucinda glanced at me, expecting me to call that a lie. But Bill was freelancing outside city limits, he was with me, a noncop; and the shooting had started unexpectedly. I tipped my head to admit that Bill had never identified himself.

Bob said to me, "I looked at the security monitor and saw two guys with guns in the dark coming toward the production trailer. I figured they were Hannah's brothers. At first, I didn't know it was you, Joe. I swear I didn't."

Tuan Le came out of the bathroom and put on khakis, loafers, and a white oxford-cloth shirt. He went to Lucinda and stood close to her. "Are you going to charge me with anything, Officer?"

She gritted her teeth, then said, "Get the hell out of here."

"Very well." He turned to Bob, said, "Ciao," and stepped out into the rain.

I asked Bob, "Why didn't you tell me you left Club Nine with him on the night Hannah got killed?"

He looked straight at me, as though he wanted to deny his relationship with Tuan. "I didn't."

"Tuan says you did. So does the bartender at Club Nine."

He yawned. It was a fake yawn—a yawn that meant, You're way off track, and you're boring me with your theories. But he said, "You know, I was in love with Hannah. I'm forty-three years old, and that was the first time I'd been in love. When she left that night, I could have killed her. It hurt that bad. But Tuan talked to me, and"—he smiled a little, like he found it funny—"he reminds me of Hannah. He sounds like her when he talks. He smells like her, too. I brought Hannah here the first night I met her. Tonight was the first time I brought Tuan." The room had nothing going for it unless you liked carpet that showed vinyl through the holes, but you would never have guessed it by the wistful way he looked around. "You know, about seven years ago, I lived in this place full-time. I was mostly out of work. And then I ran into the judge and he hired me to work at his company. He saved my life. He called it 'loyalty among old friends.'" He looked at me accusingly and said it again. "Loyalty."

"Old friends don't lie to each other, and they don't shoot each other."

He shook his head. "They lie to each other all the time. That's how they get to be old friends. And I didn't shoot you. I could have killed you easy. I saw you on the stairway before I shot the detective. But I recognized you, and I didn't shoot."

I didn't know if he was telling the truth, but a shiver rippled up my neck. "So why did you shoot the judge?"

"I already told you. I didn't."

"Yeah, and you also told me old friends lie all the time. You want to know my theory?"

"Do I have a choice?"

"I figure the judge believed in you at first. He knew about the earlier charges—that you threatened a girl-friend with a knife—and he knew about you slashing Hannah's robe on-camera. But the charges were dropped, and, hey, a video's just pretend, and little Bobby Piedras from the old neighborhood couldn't possibly be a killer. So he believed you. Odds were against you, but he always liked the long shot.

"Then came the night at Stoyz. You were delivering videos, and the Le brothers popped out of the storage room, looking for blood. Chinh came at you with a knife. But you were carrying a pistol, and you didn't let him get to you. You dropped the videos and shot. You missed the Le brothers, but poor Mr. Hassan was standing in the way, and he took two bullets.

"Okay, so now you really were a killer, but the judge

could have reasoned that it happened in self-defense—an understandable killing. Any Cub Scout could have done it. Even Bobby Piedras.

"And then a bad thing happened. You shot a cop. The judge was willing to bet on a long shot, but he was no idiot. He began to have doubts about you. You were no longer welcome at his house. That's why you weren't there when I went back to see him. And because he still didn't know what role I might be playing in your games, he tried to put me on a short chain, held by Donald Sanke's chief goon, Ben Turner.

"You started to worry, too. Without the judge's money and legal support, what would you have? But you held on to see what would happen. And you stayed at Tuan Le's apartment because that's where the judge told you to stay. A lucky break for you, since things were heating up between you and Tuan, right? Lucky until the judge figured out something was going on between the two of you. A dead girl, a dead shop owner, a wounded cop, and then hanky-panky with the dead girl's brother. That was enough for the judge. He told you he was cutting you loose. You left Tuan's apartment, figuring that distance would make things right again with the judge. But the damage was done.

"What did you do? You drove to the Dunes to confront the judge. He wouldn't budge. You argued. You shot him. End of theory."

Bob had listened politely. "It's a pretty theory. Wrong, but pretty. It explains everything except what really happened."

"Okay," I said, "what really happened?"

The room door swung open. Maybe Tuan had decided he couldn't bear to be apart from Bob. Maybe he figured Bob should have an attorney beside him before he started telling what had really happened.

Chinh and Lanh stepped into the room. They were drenched from the rain. Chinh held his knife; Lanh held a pistol.

Bob lunged for the top of the bed, reached between the headboard and the mattress, and came out with a gun.

Lucinda spun and yelled, "Drop the weapons!"

But Lanh fired at Bob, hitting the mattress, the wall. Bob fired and hit Lanh in the chest, Chinh in the head. Lanh kept coming, firing wildly, emptying his gun into the mattress, the headboard, the wall. Lucinda shouted into the gunfire, "Put it down! Put it down!" and I shouted, "Stop! Goddamn it, stop!" The noise of our voices meant so much less than the noise of the guns. Chinh flew back against a lamp, dead. Blood burst into the air from Bob's right leg. Lanh fell forward onto the foot of the bed and stayed there. Lucinda and I stood in the silence, waving our guns at everyone except each other. No one needed shooting anymore.

Bob was groping at his leg, searching for the wound causing all that blood, trying to stop the river that was flowing out of it.

He looked up and whispered, "Help."

Neither of us went to him.

"Please," he begged. "Help me."

I looked at him long and hard. Lucinda did, too. I figured it would be simple to walk away and let him bleed to death. When the old motel owner checked on the room in a day or two, he would find three bodies. Police forensics would show exactly what had happened: Bob had killed the Le brothers, and Lanh had killed Bob. No one would be confused by the triple homicide. The Le brothers were avenging their sister's death, and Bob was fighting it out to the end. It was clean and easy, and it felt right. No messy objections from lawyers and judges, no one getting off charges on technicalities or claims of self-defense.

I turned and started out of the room. Lucinda must have been thinking thoughts like mine, because she followed me.

Bob struggled across the bed and grabbed the phone, punched 911. But I went to the night table and yanked the phone line out of the wall.

"I'm bleeding bad, Joe. You walk away from me now, you're killing me."

"What's the difference?"

"I'm innocent."

I looked him in the eyes. I didn't believe him, but his eyes stopped me. I don't know why. Maybe because they were wounded eyes. Maybe because they had desperation that wasn't either innocent or guilty, just human, and that still meant something to me.

I took the pillowcase off a pillow, twisted it, and made a tourniquet. Then I stopped the Mississippi that was pouring from his leg. Lucinda and I took him to the hospital. We saved his life. I don't know why.

TWENTY-NINE

SATURDAY, 4:30 A.M., LUCINDA SAT behind an inch-thick stack of reports in an office at the District Eighteen station. Me, I just had time and nowhere else I needed to go, so I was keeping her company and verifying any details that needed verifying.

Cops came by and knocked gently on the door, as though they were coming to pay last respects, but instead they congratulated her on the arrest. A couple of them nodded hello to me, and one even told me I'd done a good job, too, but for most of them, I wasn't even there. That was okay. I acted like they weren't there, either.

We worked through a pot of coffee, and someone brought a box of Dunkin' Donuts. But my gut started churning for something solid. I was thinking about a double breakfast special from Grandma's Kitchen when Lucinda put down her pen and stared at me.

The words came hard, but she said them. "I don't like it. Do you?"

"Like what?" I said.

She picked up the report. "All of this. Piedras for the three homicides."

I was tired. I was hungry. I didn't want to think about it anymore. "No," I admitted, "it doesn't add up."

"We probably can make it stand in court, but it's not right. He was with Tuan Le when Hannah got murdered, right? He denies it, and I'll bet no one can prove it, but I know what I see. So cross him off for Hannah's murder. What remains?"

"Ahmed Hassan?"

"Yeah, Bob's there for that homicide, and he's got a gun and he's shooting it. But let's say you got it right the first time, when we were talking to the Le brothers at BlackLite. Let's say Lanh or Chinh shot the bullets that ended up in Hassan, and Piedras shot only the slug that we took out of the door frame."

I thought about it. "When can you get the ballistics results comparing the Hassan bullets with the guns Bob and the Le brothers used in the motel room?"

"Tomorrow. Maybe the day after."

"Okay, so let's say we cross off Hassan. What about the judge?"

"What about him?" she said. "Does Piedras gain anything by killing him? Only if the judge threatens to go to the district attorney with information on him. But if we eliminate Hannah and Ahmed Hassan, the judge doesn't have much to go to the district attorney with.

And, even if he did, from what you've told me, that doesn't sound like something the judge would do. If we cross Piedras off for Ahmed Hassan and Hannah, I say cross him off for the judge, too."

I nodded. It didn't make me happy.

She said, "At least we've got him solid for shooting Bill. We'll cook him for that."

I shook my head. "If the other stuff collapses, he'll walk on that one. You heard him describe the shooting. His description was accurate. Bill didn't say he was a cop. It'll look like self-defense to a jury. Bob might get probation. If he can keep Donald Sanke on his case, he might even come out of this a hero: the private man protecting himself against a zealous cop."

"So what do we do?"

"Think about it some more."

We sat and thought. I yawned. Lucinda closed her eyes, opened them again.

"I'm too tired to think," she said.

"We've still got the video of Bob slashing Hannah in the ceremonial robe."

"Yeah, but that's pretend. It's fantasy."

"And if the prosecutor shows it to the jury, they'll convict Bob of Hannah's murder even if he and Tuan Le swear they spent the night cuddling."

She nodded. "So who stabbed Hannah?"

I thought some more. "Someone who saw the video and wanted to frame Bob?"

"Who?"

I shook my head. "Except for Chinh and Lanh, just about everyone loves him."

"What about the other girlfriend, the one who accused him of threatening her with a knife?"

"Worth a look. You got that file?"

She dug through the papers on her desk and came up with a thin folder.

I could have stopped after I read the first line, naming the accused and the complainant. But I settled into my chair and read about Bob threatening the complainant with a hunting knife in the front seat of his car, about him making her have oral sex with him there, then leading her inside her home at knife point and making her have sex with him again.

I believed about half of what I read, and when I finished, I was shaking so hard inside that I planted my feet on the floor so Lucinda wouldn't see. I pretended to keep reading until the shaking stopped, and then I pretended to read some more.

Then I phoned for the home number of the Beverly Shores police detective Lori Rolison. She answered the phone on the first ring. If I woke her, she was sleeping about as deep as a coiled spring.

I said, "What did you find when you searched Carla Pakorian's car?"

"Pardon me?"

"This is Joe Kozmarski. You asked me to give her a ride home. You wanted to search her car. What did you find?"

"Searching her car without a warrant would be illegal."

"I know. What did you find?"

She gave me a long pause. "Gunshot residue."

"And?"

"We're running SEM-EDA tests to see if we can match the residue on Judge Rifkin's wound. I don't know what we'll come up with. The pool chlorine washed him pretty clean."

I still was impressed. "You're about a day ahead of me on this."

"I'm years ahead of you, Mr. Kozmarski."

"That could be true. What made you suspect her?"

"She said the judge didn't spend the night of the murder with her. But when I saw her car at the judge's house, I sent an officer over to talk to her neighbors. A groundskeeper said the judge's SUV was parked outside her condo most of the night."

"What made you send the officer to talk to him?"

"Just good police work, Mr. Kozmarski."

I hated her efficiency. "What if you can't match the residue? Do you have enough to arrest her?"

"Probably not. But we're working day and night."

"You ever sleep?"

"Every other Sunday, unless the fish are biting."

Lucinda had her gun on and a jacket in her hand by the time I hung up.

We drove toward the Dunes in a steady rain, and the sun came up behind a sky so thick with clouds, it looked like it would stay gray forever.

Carla's green A-frame was dark. If she'd kept drinking and stayed up as late the night before as I figured she had, her lights wouldn't go on till noon at the earliest.

Lori Rolison had returned the red Nissan after she'd searched it, and it was parked now in a space outside the condo.

Lucinda pulled into the space next to it. I put my hand on her arm. "Let me go in alone, okay?"

She didn't ask me what there was between Carla and me. She said, "I'll be sitting right here. Come get me if you need me."

I ran through the rain to the front door. When Carla had called the night before, she'd said she would leave the door unlocked for me so I could come in and nibble on her until she woke up. A big part of me wanted to be wrong about her. I took a minute to deal with that part of me, to quiet it, and guard the rest of myself against it so it couldn't hurt me. Then I tried the doorknob. Un-locked.

I pulled out my Glock and walked in.

She sat on the couch in the living room, looking through the picture-glass window as the gray rain brightened with dawn over the sand dunes. She had on a short white nightgown unbuttoned to the belly. The room was cold, but she didn't seem to notice. She drank coffee from a mug, though two empty bottles of Beefeater stood on the rug next to the couch.

She didn't turn to look at me as I came up beside her. "It's about time you got here, you bastard," she said.

"I got real busy," I replied.

"All night long, I waited for you. I drank, and I lis-tened to the rain falling on the roof. I wanted you so bad. So bad. The rain and the dark made me think about your touch on my skin. It hurt, you know? And now look"—she pointed at the picture window and the gray light as if it had betrayed her—"it's morning. But it's still raining. You think it'll ever stop?"

"Don't know. Why did you do it?"

"Long story." She shrugged. Then she opened her legs. "You want to go to my bedroom, or do you want me here?"

My gun was tightly in my fist; my hand sweated against it. My throat was tight. "No," I managed to say.

A tear rolled down her face. "That's what I thought." She crossed her arms over her breasts and gripped her upper arms, digging her fingertips into the bruises, as if she were trying to keep herself from flying apart.

I said, "At the judge's house yesterday morning, you told me you came because you were worried about him. You'd tried calling him but didn't get an answer. But I listened to his answering machine. There was just one message, a business call: a town engineer rescheduling some work the judge was going to do. If you were so worried, why didn't you leave a message?"

"Some things, you've got to do in person."

"Why did you go back to his house? What had you forgotten when you killed him?"

Her nails cut into her skin. If she'd gripped herself any harder, she would have bled. But she laughed—a dirty, hollow laugh—and said, "Nothing, as it turned out. I thought I'd left a jacket in his bedroom. I hadn't. It was in my kitchen. Pretty dumb."

I shook my head. "Pretty inevitable. You panic. You start worrying about what you left behind. Nothing's going to stop you from checking."

"I didn't panic." The smallest smile formed on her lips. Her grip on her arms loosened. "I never panic. I felt very calm."

"Why did you shoot him? Did he figure out that you killed Le Thi Hanh?"

Her fingers dug into her skin again.

"Or did he just refuse to tell you where Bob was hiding?"

She closed her eyes, as if trying to block out the gray light of the day, as though she was safe as long as she was surrounded by the dark of night. "What do you expect? The bitch took Bob from me. A girl shouldn't do that."

"You followed her from Club Nine to the Hilton and stabbed her in the hotel room."

"More or less."

"And you made it look like the video where Bob slashes her, so the cops would think he did it."

"I'm not always dumb." She started rocking gently from side to side.

"The only thing I don't get is the couple. How did you know they wouldn't identify you?"

The little smile. "I knew them, silly. I had them pick her up at the club."

Silly. Me. A silly bastard. "Who were they?"

She shook her head.

I pointed my gun at her. "Who?"

A man's voice spoke from the dark beyond the bedroom door. "One of them was me." The bald guy with the shotgun stepped into the living room. He had a bandage wrapped around his forehead, blood seeping through, courtesy of the Saturn steering wheel. His shotgun was pointed at my chest. I figured if I spun and shot him in the head, maybe I could escape getting killed. Chances weren't great, but I was thinking about them when his tall, skinny partner stepped out of the kitchen with a pistol.

Carla said, "No, I'm not always dumb."

I shook my head. "If I had a gold star for clever crazy people, I would stick it on your forehead. How did you get these goons to come after me downtown?"

"How do you think? Most men do what I want them to."

She had a point. "But not Bob," I said.

"No. The bastard." And her voice turned vicious. "And not you, either."

"Put down your gun," the skinny man said.

I looked him up and down. "I could shoot her," I offered.

"Put down the gun or we shoot *you*," said the bald one.

I gently set my gun on the coffee table.

"And now?" The bald man was asking Carla.

She didn't need to think about the answer. "Kill him."

The bald man lowered his eye to the shotgun sight and drew a bead on me.

"Why do you want to kill me?" I said to Carla. "Why did you send them after me to begin with?"

"You said on the phone that you were getting the information you needed to figure this out. I got nervous. I thought you knew about me. And now you do." She rocked from side to side again. "You should be flattered.

I thought it would take three guys to bring you down. I underestimated you—for a little while."

"Don't do this," I said.

"Do it," she said to the bald man.

As he squeezed the trigger, Lucinda kicked open the front door, arms extended, hands clasped around her pistol as if she were praying to something between heaven and hell. She shot the bald man twice in the head. The sound was huge. The shotgun went off, and the blast went straight into the beams high in the A-frame. The bald man fell. I dived for my gun, had it in my hand before I hit the floor, and shot the other man. I aimed for his skinny chest, but I hit him in the head.

Carla didn't move from the couch. She didn't look worried. She was beyond worry.

I lay on the floor and gazed up at Lucinda. "You said you were going to stay in the car."

"I lied."

"Always lie to me," I said.

THIRTY

MONDAY, CORRINE AND I went to the judge's funeral. I had slept all Saturday afternoon and most of the day Sunday, then gone to Mom's for dinner. Afterward, Mom drove me and Jason to the airport, and I sprang my car from short-term parking. The two hundred dollars I paid for three days was about what I would have gotten if I had sold my old Skylark for scrap, but sometimes you pay to keep the things you know and love. I took Jason home. I didn't tell him about Friday night, and he didn't ask, even though it was all over the news. But he looked at me as if he knew it was tough. I suppose some eleven-year-olds can do that if they've seen enough tough times themselves.

The judge's funeral started at ten. I didn't cry; I'd done all my crying for him already. I sat next to Corrine and thought about the living—about her, about Jason—and I almost forgot about the dead. Just seven other people showed up to see the judge off. One was his lawyer—not Donald Sanke, but a cigar-smoking guy named Stan Sarnowski. One was another ex-judge, who'd gone to prison in the corruption sting. His suit looked forty years old, and he smelled like sweat and whiskey. One was the town manager from Berwyn, who'd canceled out on the judge on the morning of his murder. The other four were fishing pals of various sizes and shapes. Corrine was the only woman there.

Even though I was glad to be with Corrine, I sometimes slipped and started thinking about Lucinda. After I'd gotten Jason to bed on Sunday night, I had talked with her on the phone. "I'm getting some heat for working out of jurisdiction," she had said. "Franklin Park's no big deal, but Beverly Shores looks like trouble. I shouldn't be shooting my service pistol across the state line."

"You saved my life."

"They say I shouldn't have been there to begin with."

"They don't know what they're talking about."

She had been at the hospital to see Bill, and he was looking good. He would get to go home midweek, and he'd already sent Annie back to Ohio. "But word is that Piedras isn't doing so well," she'd said. "He'll survive, but his leg is shattered."

"The kids at Club Nine will have to dance without him. What do you hear on Carla Pakorian?"

"She's telling her story to anyone who will listen, and the public defender is threatening to quit."

I didn't ask if she had mentioned my part in the story.

———

MONDAY MORNING, I'D GOTTEN Jason dressed and fed him a couple Eggos. Then I'd driven him to school, dropped him off in front like all the kids who had moms or dads. The sky was still gray, and mist was falling, but it didn't seem to bring him down. He socked me in the shoulder with a grin before he got out. I don't know where he learned to do that; probably something he saw on TV. I rubbed the spot where he socked me. I liked the feel of it.

Then I drove home and changed into a suit, and Corrine picked me up for the judge's last party. He had a plot under an oak tree in Calvary Cemetery, facing Lake Michigan as Sheridan Road curved out of the north side of the city. They lowered him into it in a soft rain. He would spend eternity hearing rush-hour traffic twice a day and the crash of waves in between. Sarnowski tapped me on the shoulder as we left the cemetery. "I was looking over the will last night," he said. "He left you his fishing boat."

Corrine gave me a smile for that, like it was a sign from God, or at least from the judge, that I should get in touch with my inner fisherman, and start loving her better, too.

"I don't want anything owned by the judge," I said.

"It's yours to do whatever you want," said Sarnowski.

"Then I'll set it on a course toward the middle of the lake and light it on fire. The deeper it sinks, the better."

Corrine gave me a look that said I was a fool.

"For fifteen years, I lived under the weight of the judge's lies," I said. "Now he's gone. Why should I let the weight drag on me?"

"Because it's a free boat, damn it," she said. "A free boat."

"You've got a point, but I still don't want the thing." Sarnowski scooted away.

Corrine frowned. "You're not going to change, are you?"

"Why do you say that?"

"You dream about spending your days fishing, and now a fishing boat falls out of the sky and hits you on the head, and you don't want it."

"My dream is to do it my way, not the judge's."

"And not *my* way."

"I didn't say that."

"You didn't need to. When will you cut back and relax? When will you make time for me?"

"You want an exact date?"

"Yes," she said. "An exact date."

"I don't know exactly. Soon. After I clean things up."

She laughed. There was scorn in the laugh.

"You really don't want me to give this up," I said. "I know there're times when it seems like a good idea. But if you cut away too much of me, I'm gone. I'll follow you around like a little poodle, licking your ankles and begging for a treat. I'll be no trouble at all. For a while, it'll be nice. But sooner or later, you want to kick a dog like that."

"You know why I want you to change? Because you say things like that."

I thought about that as we drove away from the cemetery. I said, "Look, I want you in my life. I love you, and I need you."

"I know," she said. "But don't *you* know? Things will never be clean. No matter how well you scrub, there's always dirt left over. You've got to learn to live with that."

"You're right—"

"But—"

But everything, I thought. "But nothing."

She gave me a gentle smile.

We pulled to the curb in front of my house.

"Will you come inside?"

"Is the kid at school?"

The kid. "Yeah, Jason's at school."

"Yeah," she said, "I'll come inside."

In the living room, I ran my finger down her cheek, down her neck, into the gap between her breasts. Her skin was cool, damp from the September rain, and she leaned into my warmth. We kissed.

I said, "After everything, you're the only one for me."

She looked me in the eyes, and our closeness blurred my vision. "I know." She held my shirt below the collar and backed toward the couch, sat slowly, pulled me down over her. We kissed. She pulled me toward her. We fell sideways on the couch, our arms, legs, and bodies together. But then she stopped kissing me and reached behind her head. We had rolled onto Jason's baseball glove.

We both laughed. "What about Jason?" I said.

She smiled. "He's a cute kid."

"Yeah," I said. "And he needs something like this."

"Like you, you mean."

I nodded. "Like me."

"How long?"

"Exact dates?"

"No." The smile stayed. "Your best guess."

"I don't know. A couple months, maybe longer." I was thinking, Probably forever.

"I don't know, Joe."

"He needs someone like you, too. If you would be with us."

She nodded slowly, considering it.

"I love you," I said.

She pulled away from me. "I love you, too. That's the damn problem."

"Don't let it be a problem. Let's not let it be." I took her hand and kissed it.

She looked unhappy. "I've got to go now, okay?"

I held her hand. "Do you want this?"

"Yeah, I want this. That's why I followed you inside. It's why I don't stay away from you."

"Then stay."

She pulled her hand out of mine. "I can't right now. I can't." She got up and went to the door.

I watched from the window as she climbed into her car. She kissed two fingers and waved them at me, then pulled from the curb.

I went into the kitchen and looked at the table. Jason's plate was still there. He'd left half a waffle in a pool of syrup, a glass of milk. I sat down and tried to think things through, but I had no idea what Corrine really wanted, what I really wanted.

Then the doorbell rang. I laughed. Corrine had come back, I thought, just because I asked her to stay. It was simple. Sometimes you don't need to think things through. Sometimes you just have to let them happen and make whatever mess they make. Sometimes you shouldn't think.

I opened the front door. Lucinda stood on the front step. She was wearing jeans and a white T-shirt, no coat. Her hair was wet from the rain. Her eyes were red.

"They put me on administrative leave," she said. "Unpaid. They say they're going to demote me."

"They can't do that. They can't just—"

"I know," she said. "But they did. They'll have a hearing, yeah. But it's done. I'm done."

I knew she was right. From the moment she pulled the trigger in Beverly Shores, her fast-track job was gone. We'd celebrated, and the papers had made her out as a hero. But you don't break as many rules as she broke and get away with it. We'd cleaned up three homicides, but Corrine was right: Even the best cleanup leaves dirt behind. This time, there was a lot of dirt. A lot of blood. The higher-ups in the police department took their uniforms to the dry cleaner's. They kept a crease in their pant legs. The toes of their shoes sparkled in the sun. They liked it clean. Lucinda's part in this case was too much dirt and blood for them.

"Come in," I said.

She did, and I closed the door behind her.

She stood close to me, wet from the rain, exhausted from the past week. And then she was in my arms and we were kissing. I don't remember how. We walked down the hall to my bedroom. I don't know how. I don't know why.